I0591413

Metaphorosis

June 2022

Beautifully made speculative fiction

Also from Metaphorosis

Metaphorosis Magazine

Metaphorosis: Best of 20xx
Metaphorosis 20xx: The Complete Stories
annual issues, from 2016

Monthly issues

Plant Based Press

Best Vegan Science Fiction & Fantasy
annual issues, 2016-2020

from B. Morris Allen:
Chambers of the Heart: speculative stories
Susurrus
Allenthology: Volume I
Tocsin: and other stories
Start with Stones: collected stories
Metaphorosis: a collection of stories

Verdage

Reading 5X5 x2: Duets
Score – an SFF symphony
Reading 5X5: Readers' Edition
Reading 5X5: Writers' Edition

Vestige

The Nocturnals, by Mariah Montoya

Metaphorosis

June 2022

edited by
B. Morris Allen

ISSN: 2573-136X (online)
ISBN: 978-1-64076-230-5 (e-book)
ISBN: 978-1-64076-231-2 (paperback)

Metaphorosis
a magazine of speculative fiction
from
Metaphorosis Publishing

Neskowin

June 2022

Since We Don't Have Wings

Gwen Whiting

Chash sloshed through the mud on his way home, picking up bits of glass and hiding them in his pockets. His breath quickened every time he saw the sparkle of glass and he veered toward it, picking up every colored shard he found.

"Chash!" He ignored the voice. *Maybe he'll go away if I don't respond.* It didn't work. Norio caught up to him easily, despite the bag he carried. "Picking up glass here again? Can't believe there's any left for you to take."

"There isn't much," he mumbled. "Nothing wrong with taking it. No one's lived here since the war ended." They were both too young to clearly remember the night that the village had burnt while firebirds slashed through the skies overhead. What stories Chash knew had been woven into his mind by eavesdropping on elders who could not forget.

"If you say so." Norio said. "Just buy your glass from the peddler. He'll be coming down the coast soon."

Chash's face flamed.

"Oh, right. I forgot. You can't afford it." Norio shoved his bag at Chash. "Here. This is the reason I came after you. My mother sends food."

"We don't need it." His cheeks were still hot, but he didn't take the food.

"She insists. Says we still owe you from something Besu did during the war." Norio lifted the bag up, holding it now just out of Chash's reach. "Maybe if you take it, I won't catch you digging through the mud looking for glass to sharpen your kite strings."

It was rude not to take a gift freely offered and his grandmother, Besu, would be furious if he refused on their behalf. Even if she insisted on giving away much of the food they had, saying that others needed it more.

"Tell your mother thanks," he muttered, reaching for the bag.

Norio jerked it back.

"What? I didn't hear you."

"I said, thank you." Chash reached again, but this time, Norio stepped back and dropped the bag. Jassa fruits spilled out, their tender flesh breaking as they hit the ground. The bright orange skins were now coated in mud.

Chash dropped his gaze, staring down at his feet. Norio wanted him to kneel in the dirt, to watch him pick up the ruined fruit, but he wouldn't. Not where Norio could see.

"You just going to let it rot?"

Chash said nothing.

"Some kite fighter you're going to be." Norio said. "Good luck at Festival." Chash lifted his head as Norio ground a fruit down with the heel of his boot, then left. He waited for Norio to be completely out of sight before grabbing the dropped bag and filling it with fruit. None of this would matter once it was time for the festival.

The Festival of Wings was only four days away and it was how Chash planned to make his fortune. The event wasn't focused on birds, but on kites. Huge as a man or small as a dove. Painted like a rainbow or glossy black. Made from paper, silk, linen, even hair.... No one agreed on what made the strongest kite or the fastest. But when the kite fights began, the owner of the last kite in the air earned the emperor's favor. With his favor came a position in the imperial army and the chance to control one of the mighty firebirds who were reborn when killed in battle.

Daydreams lightened Chash's step as he continued home, turning past the magistrate's house. One of the windows was smashed. As the festival drew near, the poorest fighters in Santao broke windows to steal glass to coat their kite strings. He kept his head down. If Norio saw him here, he'd probably tell someone Chash was breaking windows now.

When he reached their cottage, Chash opened the door and crept inside quietly to avoid disturbing his grandmother's work. She was hunched over a swatch of green silk, hemming a sleeve with golden thread.

"You're late." Besu set her needle down, then stretched her fingers. The skin around her eyes was red, and as she blinked, tears glimmered on her lashes. She hadn't lit any of the candles at her table, even though the sun and moon were changing places. *She needs to stop sewing after sunset. She'll go blind if she doesn't.* Chash frowned. Suggesting to Besu that she stop sewing would have been like asking her to stop breathing.

"I wish you wouldn't work so hard." Chash emptied his pockets onto the table. He pulled the fabric inside out and shook it to keep glass slivers from surprising his fingers later.

"Mmm." She rocked back in her chair as he lit the lamps. "Festival's coming. And Lia pays well. She won't be happy if her dress isn't the finest in four villages."

"If I win the fights this year, you won't ever have to sew a dress again."

"My hands like to sew. It's my eyes that don't care for it."

"I'll help you finish the dresses after dinner." Chash stoked the fire. He set a pot of water to boil and began preparing dinner. Other men in the village didn't cook or sew, but Besu had insisted he learn. It was only fair, she said, to take turns. After he had finished making the soup and setting the table, he sat down with Besu to eat. "I was on Manu's crew for the fishing today. Said he saw a waterhorse in the waves."

"They say waterhorse hair makes the best kite strings," Besu commented. "But try catching one."

He laughed.

"Manu put out a trap before we left. If there is a waterhorse, it'll be too clever for it. He hasn't caught one yet." The tender bitterness of the sana root, only edible in the spring, washed over Chash's tongue as he sipped at the edge of his bowl.

"Are you thinking of hunting waterhorse tonight?" Besu slurped her soup, squinting at him. A few drops splattered on the table, but she didn't notice. "You'll need a net for it. And be sure to take one of the lanterns."

"I promised to help you sew." Hours of embroidering tiny flowers for village women lay ahead. Chash had to be her eyes in the dim light to help her manage such delicate work, even as his own eyes watered and burned from lack of sleep.

"I'm a bit behind. Otherwise, I'd weave you something to catch the hair with. No need to harm the poor creature." She set her bowl down, still half-full. "We should get to work. Maybe some of the hair will wash up on the beach. You can pick it off the rocks and I'll dry it."

He sighed and cleared the table. Fishing began at dawn and there weren't many hours left in the night.

The days spent fishing were long and hard. Chash's shoulders ached after pulling in heavy ropes, and when it stormed, the very sea itself battered already-bruised muscles. Manu had sent him to mend nets that day, an easier task than working on the boats. The waterhorse had not been caught the night before, but had thrashed around before it escaped into deeper waters, snarling and snapping the weave with its teeth.

He sat on an overturned barrel near the prow of the ship, tugging and testing the flax of the net as he searched for places that the waterhorse had broken. Chash plucked out strands of silky green hair that the beast had left behind and secreted them in his pocket. Other crew members hoisted sails while Chash fixed the nets, the rank smell of fish oil and pitch wafting toward him with every light breeze. As he worked, he caught snatches of conversations from the stern.

"...that waterhorse." Norio's voice floated over on the breeze.

"Old Manu'll never catch it. All he's ever gotten is bits of hair. Lucky for Chash the old man picked him to tend the nets. Not that he'll scavenge enough to string a spool." Aran replied.

Chash paused when he heard his name.

"Can't believe he sews his own kites." Norio said. "Even if he's good with a needle."

"Women make kites, men fly them," Aran agreed. "Used to be that way, anyhow. Won't be long and we'll have girls working on the docks."

"Besu doesn't make kites. I tried getting her to sew one for me once."

"Too bad, that. She's the finest seamstress in the village."

"Well, Besu must not think Chash can win. Otherwise, she'd sew him a kite," Norio said.

"Can you imagine him trying to rein in a firebird?" Aran's laugh bellowed. "He can barely haul a net up with those arms." The two men laughed together, and others joined in.

Chash threw the net down and stood, his hand balling into a fist. *This again. If they want me to prove I'm strong, I'll prove it.* A broad hand clapped down on his shoulder, then shoved him back down on his stool.

It was Manu.

"I think I hear sirens across the water. Thought you might need these to protect against the singing." Manu handed two lumps of wax, dented by the heat of his hand, to Chash.

"Thank you." Chash hunched over, staring at his feet.

Manu grunted, then walked off.

When I win the fight and go to battle for the emperor, they'll see. Hauling fish doesn't make a man. Chash shoved the plugs in his ears, muting Norio's laughter, and kept working.

Besu's table was piled high with cotton and silk that night, and Chash lit three candles at a time when they both should have been sleeping. Chash picked up a dress the color of weak tea, thrusting his needle into the cotton. After a moment, his grandmother reached out, fumbling for his hand, and took the cloth away.

"What did that dress ever do to you?" she muttered. Her fingers ran across the rippling fabric, her thumb pausing at a puckered hem. "Your stitches are crooked. And knots, Chash! The thread is loose where it should be tight and here – here – here – I shouldn't feel anything at all." Her shoulders heaved and she dropped it on the table.

She had always commented before on how the evenness of his stitches looked and how the colors of one pattern complemented another, not the way the material felt.

"Ah — here. Take it back and pull the stitches out. Carefully, Chash. There's only enough of that color for one dress and who knows if the peddler will come before Festival." Besu handed the sleeve back to him, her tired eyes puffed into swollen slits. "I wish you'd give up the fishing. There's plenty of work to be had in Santao for two tailors."

"You always ask that." He took the sleeve back and picked up a small knife to rip out the stitches. "I want to do something bigger; will anyone care how well I hem a sleeve after I'm dead?"

"I've sewn for this village for generations. My mother before me and her mother before her. The people wear our clothing on their back when they marry, when they fight, when they die. They pass on our best dresses to their daughters, wrap their babies in the blankets that we stitch together from old clothes. Our family will be remembered."

"Your mother, her mother," Chash said. "Never any fathers doing the work."

"They didn't have the talent or the patience. But you do." Besu clamped her lips together for a moment, then asked, "How is it different from mending nets? Men do that. You do that."

All the hours of mending flax echoed in his bones as she spoke, how cord tightened around his fingers when he worked, smelling of seaweed, sand, and the stink of the tides. The way that the ocean seeped into his skin and roughed his fingers so that silk now snagged on his knuckles when he sewed at night. Working on the rough waters aged men until even their minds grew calloused and hard.

"How is it different?" she repeated.

"I don't know. It just is." Chash threaded a new needle. He stabbed the sleeve hard enough to pucker the fabric, but Besu didn't stop him. Was it because she didn't want to pick a fight or because she couldn't see his work?

"It's ridiculous, is what it is." She narrowed her eyes at him for a moment, then picked up her own needle. "Only reason that Manu doesn't have women mending his nets is because that might mean we'd have to be on the docks to do it. And then we'd want to fish. And after that, who knows? Maybe we wouldn't need men anymore." She snorted.

Chash didn't answer.

Besu glanced in his direction, then stopped and rubbed her eyes.

"There're only four days until Festival. Have you finished your kite?" Besu asked.

"Of course. I've been practicing for weeks when the storms aren't heavy." He wondered how a kite sewn by Besu would hold up in the wind. He wouldn't ask her to sew for him now, however, no matter what Norio said — his pride was stitched into every line and fold of the kite he had crafted.

"Hm. Bring me your kite. If you've sewn any knots into it, there'll be no flying it in a harsh wind." She clacked her tongue, but her tone warmed him. He placed the sleeve in the basket at his feet and went to collect his kite from the shelf where it rested. Sewn from a year's worth of dress scraps, its oval shape shimmered blue and orange and violet. The kite's edges were pointed, the bottom weighted with folded fabric stitched closed. The extra weight would give it strength.

Besu grazed the silk with her palms, her eyes closed as her fingers traveled the stitches and bumps of the material. Her mouth turned up into a half-moon smile, lips almost touching her eyes.

"That's one of Lia's dresses. I remember stitching those flowers." There was a little catch in her voice. "And Hana's and Zholi's. Won't they be surprised." She didn't comment on the way that the different colors clashed with one another.

She smoothed the ripples in the fabric out, still smiling.

"I made a kite from a dress once," Besu said.

"I didn't know you'd ever made kites." His forehead wrinkled. It had only been three years since women were first allowed to join the kite fights, after it was apparent that the emperor's wives would bear only daughters. The year that Akrivi won, her golden dragon kite had slashed the strings of a hundred contenders with ease. His grandmother had cried as the last kite plummeted from the sky.

"I did. And I flew them too. Just not in the fights. I — women — weren't allowed then, but I always thought I would've won. My kite was strong — and sewn from the finest fabric in three villages." His grandmother laughed, so hard that it turned into a series of loud coughs.

"How did you find the coin for that? I thought your father raised pigs." Chash patted her on the back.

"I sewed it from my wedding dress." Besu cackled.

"Your wedding dress?" His hand fell away as he gaped.

"The finest fabric to be had." Her hand caressed his kite one last time before she handed it to him.

"Oh." Besu's hands were covered with tiny nicks and scars. *Did those marks come from fighting kites?*

"I didn't love your grandfather at first and I was so angry. Marrying him meant I'd never leave Santao. If my mother had found out I'd used that dress, though..." Besu laughed. "I hid what I'd done. Just cut the inside layer of the skirt shorter — better for summer anyhow. Never told your grandfather."

Chash had never known his grandfather, nor could he remember his parents. His father had been killed in one of the emperor's wars, his mother dead of sickness a few months later, and after Besu had taken him into her home, the war had come to Santao. Firebirds shrieked overhead as his grandmother dragged him with her, pounding on door after door, then leading people into the hills to hide. Some people said the firebirds had saved them from the raiders that stormed through the village, but he knew better. It had been Besu.

"I'm sorry you never got to fight," he said.

"It was worth it, in the end. I wouldn't have made a good soldier." Besu reached out, her bony hands clasping his face for a quick squeeze. "It's time I went to bed. You need to spend time on your kite now — I'll finish the sewing in the morning." She let go of his face, then walked into the next room. His grandmother was wrong, he thought. She would have made an excellent warrior. What had the first emperor been thinking when he decided that women were not worthy of taming his precious firebirds?

The next day, Chash strapped his kite to his back for the long walk to the practice field. The far edges of it flapped past his shoulders, bits of tail breaking free from the twine binding it. He caught glimpses of blue from the corners of his eyes as he walked, never quite knowing if it was kite or sky or ocean that he saw.

Warm breezes from the eastern winds brushed his cheeks and he hummed a little as he walked. It would be a good Festival if the winds kept up and the storms stayed behind. His kite rustled as someone nudged Chash's shoulder, pushing him off the rocky path.

He stilled.

"That the kite you're fighting at Festival?" Norio said.

Chash kept walking. He didn't want trouble.

"Hey, I wanted to talk to you for a minute."

What could Norio want? Chash stopped.

"Just thought I'd say I was sorry. About the other day. The fruit." Norio edged closer. The wind had picked up and the edges of the kite on Chash's back flapped as if they longed to take flight.

"Fine," Chash muttered.

"Show me your kite. I want to see how you sew." Norio gestured to Chash's back.

"No, I don't think so." Fliers never let their competitors look at their kites this close to Festival — opponents could spot a kite's weaknesses and plan for it.

"Come on." Norio reached for the kite, grasping the edge.

Surprised, Chash turned. The fabric ripped and Norio stumbled back with rounded eyes.

Chash's chest tightened so hard that it hurt.

Turquoise silk fluttered in Norio's fist.

"No." Chash's hand trembled as he twisted his arm around, trying to feel the kite on his back. Its spine hung crooked, the edge of it snapped and slapping against his side.

"I can show you how to fix—"

"You? You're going to show me how to fix a kite? You can't even mend your own tunic."

"I don't have to. My mother does that kind of work." Norio's lip curled.

"Only because you're too stupid to figure out a pattern."

"At least I don't sit around at night and sew dresses with my grandmother." There it was. The same taunt Norio had been using since they were children. Besu told Chash to turn his back on an insult and walk away — that fighting didn't make a man — but she didn't understand. She couldn't. Over and over and over — it didn't matter what he said or where they were — Norio never stopped. Wouldn't stop unless Chash made him stop.

Chash jumped at Norio. The two men tumbled to the ground, the kite frame cracking as they rolled over dust and broken bricks. Splintered wood dug into Chash's shoulders, but he kicked at Norio, sending the other man sprawling. Norio's hand missed him, punching the air by his face.

Chash's fist plunged into Norio's stomach.

He sucked his breath in as Norio choked.

Norio's next punch connected with Chash's jaw, smacking him backward on the ground. A flash of jagged black and white squares cut across his vision before it cleared, leaving his neck stiff and his head throbbing.

Norio stood up, brushing off his trousers. He hunched over, wheezing, and offered Chash a hand up. When Chash didn't take it, Norio shrugged.

"Suit yourself." He kicked at the dirt by Chash's head as he walked away.

That night, while Besu snored on her sleeping mat, Chash spread out the pieces of his kite. The shaved bamboo of the spine and spars had splintered and broken, and the silk was ripped and torn. Earth and red brick dust was ground into the fabric, muting its many colors. Bits of waterhorse hair glistened, each one a reminder of a precious hour spent combing the beach at dawn. Even if there had been the spare money or material to craft a new kite, there was no more time.

What would it feel like to control a firebird's golden chains? To do something more than haul fish out of the ocean? Chash picked up his needle. The material rustled against his skin as what he envisioned began to take shape. He stitched and cut, using thread to create his own pictures, embroidering birds and fire against the fabric. When he finished, he leaned back in his chair.

It was no longer a kite, but it might make someone a nice hat.

He buried his head in his hands.

His grandmother shuffled to the table. Her hand warmed the back of his neck as she stroked his hair.

"I thought I'd win this year," Chash blurted.

"You still can. Look." She moved, the frigid night air quickly flooding the space her hand vacated. He lifted his head.

On the table was a kite like no other Chash had seen. It was shaped like a swan and made of the palest pink silk. Its huge wings spanned the width of his own arms. He picked it up, marveling at the tiny perfect stitches that bound it to its frame. Each bar was carefully carved, and the maker had whittled each end to a point before sliding it into tiny pockets of fabric to hold it securely. A tail of thin white ribbons floated from the end of the kite.

"You can't get spidersilk anymore," Besu said. "It was part of my dowry."

"It's beautiful." It took hours to make so many stitches so evenly — hundreds of hours spent on a kite for a woman not allowed to fly it.

"I wanted to fight kites when I was younger. They didn't allow it then. I was supposed to want to be a wife and a mother, but I didn't want any of those things. When Nemh — your mother — married, I thought I was free, but then your parents died. That night that the firebirds saved the village, I left you in the caves with Manu." Besu pressed her hands over her heart, folding her fingers into one another. "I told him I was going back to look for others, but I lied."

"Why didn't you go?" Chash asked.

"I went home first. All your things were still spread out on the floor. A blanket, an old pile of sticks you played with. A broken sandal I was mending..." Besu spoke as if his old toys were there in the room between them. "I saw those things and tried to imagine my life without you. I couldn't. So, I took the kite, and I came back."

He bowed his head.

Besu touched his shoulder, then crooked a finger under his chin to lift it.

"It was a good choice. I live on in you." She leaned back in her chair. "Since we don't have wings, we make kites. I want you to have this. My wings."

"I can't, Grandmother."

"I want to see the kite fights. To see you fight."

"You're not that old," Chash protested.

"It's my eyes that are weak, not my heart." Besu patted his hand, gesturing to the kite. "The strings... I wove them from flame reed and seagrass." He picked up a string, gingerly at first, expecting it to be coated with broken glass or woven around hidden razors. It was thick but there was no sign of hidden danger.

"There's no glass — how were you going to cut the other kites down?"

"I wasn't. I've seen sixty Festivals and at every one, there's far more wounds than winners. Look at your hands." Besu shook her head. "The last kite in the air is the one that wins. If the rope was strong and I was clever, I thought I wouldn't need to hurt anything or anyone. Maybe I could win by enduring."

His finger ran up and down the ridges of the cord. It smelled like salt and ash, just as a firebird would. *His* firebird.

"You can put your own strings on it. No need to indulge an old woman's dreams." Besu rose, patting his shoulder before lumbering back to bed. He nodded, but he tucked the string into his pocket.

On the morning of the festival, the sky was cloudless, and the breeze was light. Besu took Chash's arm and chattered away at him like a small bird as they climbed up into the wagon that traveled the road up the coastline towards the docks of Cantara. The two of them packed in with six women, most of them wearing dresses he had made. He cradled Besu's kite in his arms, wrapped up tightly in an old blanket, careful not to bump it into one of the women as the wagon rocked and swayed down the old dirt road that led away from Santao.

"Besu, I'm so glad you're coming with us to Festival this year. My husband told me that he's never seen me look so fine before." One of the women preened, holding out her arms to showcase the tiny leaves that Besu and Chash had sewn across the length of the dress. Her comments provoked a round of admiration and competition.

For once, Besu smiled and didn't comment on what the women wore, other than to thank them for their praise. Her face turned up, toward the sun, as the others sang a traveling song. Chash leaned back against the wagon's rail and let the road rock him to sleep.

A light jab woke him.

"You slept the whole way," Besu chided. With a groan, Chash rose and handed her the bundle with the kite. He hopped down from the wagon, then gently helped Besu and the kite to the ground. The faint scent of cinnamon and sugar wafted from one of the street stalls as a bee buzzed past him. No doubt it had escaped from one of the beekeepers who came to festivals, shouting about charmed honey and wax. Such small magic was costly and outlawed in the kite fights, though it was always rumored that some fighter had charmed their strings.

"Pickled limes." Besu clutched his arm. Her nose poked ahead of her feet as she sniffed the air, turning first in one direction, then another. "Where are they?"

"That way." Chash frowned. *She should be able to see that stall. It's just a few steps away.* He took the kite from her and cradled it underneath his other arm, not daring to strap it on his back.

"The sun's almost to the top of the sky. We need to hurry to the kite field." He tried to walk a little faster, but Besu struggled to keep up, squinting and wobbling with uncertainty as she walked. He slowed his pace to let her lean on him and they made their way past the longest pier in Cantara, ignoring the cries and shouts of vendors. He stopped a few times, marveling at the tiny ash-dragons that zipped between the cooking fires, and the mechanical birds that called out endearments to them both from jeweled cages. Besu jabbed a bony finger in his side, and they continued.

The field was full this year. There was a platform at the edge of it, built high above the low pastures where the fighters assembled, attaching strings, and making quick, desperate repairs. The Festival of Wings was one of twelve held around the country. Every year, Cantara prepared for the emperor's arrival, but he chose to honor richer cities. To save face, the villagers claimed that the firebirds hated the sea, and the emperor didn't travel without them.

Chash and Besu went to the field just as the crier shouted for the fighters to line up. The wind blew hard, and a few kites shot upward, their owners hurrying to wind the string back on the spool.

"Be careful," he told Besu. "Not everyone watches where their strings fly." She nodded and he realized how ridiculous it was to caution a woman who had lived through wars and floods and years of starvation. Carefully unfolding the kite, Chash removed the spools of kite strings that he carried in his pockets, wrapped up tightly in leather. Besu stared out at the field, her eyes unblinking.

She should have gotten her chance. His stomach tightened. It was an accident of birth and time that he stood here to fight using the kite that she made so many years ago.

The kite field was a battleground in miniature — the youngest fighters yelped as they slit fingers on razored strings. Men and a few women raised their kites, brilliantly colored rectangles, diamonds, and six-sided shapes thrashing in the wind. Shouts of anger and gasps of frustration echoed throughout the crowd as fighters fought for control of their lines, bringing each kite into the air for battle.

When he turned to Besu, her face was relaxed. It was then that he understood, watching her gaze toward the sounds of

Since We Don't Have Wings

fighting, rather than the kites flapping in the wind. *She can't see. Not enough to watch me fly her kite.*

I'll tell her what's happening. Make this the best fight she's ever been to. Chash knelt to fasten the lines, fighting back the sudden tightness in his throat. Someone tapped his shoulder and he looked up.

"Hey," Norio said.

"Hey, Norio." Chash didn't stand to greet him.

"Norio, I haven't seen you since you were standing at your auntie Lia's knee," Besu said. "Come here and give this old woman a hug." She smiled and gave Norio a squeeze. "Chash is getting ready for the fights — and why aren't you? Your mother says you've been practicing for weeks."

"I am — I mean, I have been." Norio said. "Could I have a minute with Chash?"

Besu looked at Chash, and he nodded.

"Well, it was good talking with you." She patted Norio's arm before weaving toward the chatter of relatives gathered near one of the younger fighters.

"What do you want?" Chash asked, watching Besu to make sure she found her way to her friends.

"I just want to say I'm sorry about the kite. About what I said."

"You've been saying it for years. Why do you care now?"

"My mother found out about our fight. She told me about the day the firebirds came to our village... I don't remember it and she never would tell me anything about the war before." Norio stared down at the ground. "Besu saved our family. I knew we owed her a debt, but I never knew why." He knotted his hands together. "Mother wants me to offer you my kite."

"What about you?" Chash asked. He'd imagined getting an apology for years. Now that he had it, he didn't feel vindicated. He just felt sad.

"I don't want to give it up," Norio admitted. "But I'm the one who broke your kite. I'm the one who has to make it right, not my family."

If I take his kite, he can't fight. Part of him wanted to agree and take the kite so Norio would regret the hundreds of small insults that rested between them. But how could he face Besu if he won the battle by taking away Norio's ability to fight?

"Besu's losing her sight," he said. "She asked me to fly her kite. It might be the last time she sees the fights. Keep your kite — we'll meet in the air."

"I knew she was going blind, but..." Norio stopped, then reached out and offered Chash his hand. "Thank you." The two men shook hands and wished each other luck. Chash picked up his spool again as Besu came back to their spot, slowly navigating across the field.

If I win, what happens to her? There was glory in going to war. It would change him into a man. His fingers hesitated over the shattered glass strings. *But what kind of man would I be?* He was tired of fighting insults with fists. It felt good to forgive.

He set his own spool down, ignoring the blood on his fingertips. Besu was nearly blind — to control a string coated in crushed glass would challenge her. He looped the cord she had made around a new spool, then fastened it to the spine of the kite.

"Come." He took Besu's arm. The crier shouted, warning spectators away from the fight. The field emptied out as men, women, and children retreated toward the platform, forming a small crowd around its outer perimeter.

"Only the fighters are allowed to stay on the field until the kites are in the air," Besu chided him.

"I know." Chash pulled her to the center of the field, ignoring the confused faces of the other fighters. She peered at him, then at the line that the fighters had made with their bodies. He pushed the spool into her hands. "I used your strings. I'll help you guide it."

A horn blew in the distance and the line broke, each fighter running with their kite until the wind caught it, taking it aloft. Chash and Besu ran last, his hand over hers as they hobbled together, four clumsy legs stumbling over grass and mud.

"We won't win," she shouted, laughing.

"That's not true!" The kite had soared up to the clouds, its silken wings spread high. They stopped, holding the spool in both their hands. Besu's head swiveled and finally stopped, but she wasn't looking in the right direction. Another kite snaked toward theirs, shaped like a red box. The lines of it glittered when the sun caught it.

She whispered, her head down, "I can't see it. All I see is clouds."

"Then I'll tell you what's happening." Chash kept one hand steady on hers and helped her spin the spool, pulling the string taut. The red kite neared. It swooped down toward the swan, and he reached out with his free hand to keep the line steady.

"I feel something," she said.

"There's another kite near us. It's red and the corner is a bit crinkled. I think it's paper." The swan caught the wind, its wings billowing out with the breeze, as the red kite swirled, dancing on the breeze. The sparkling glass lines drew his eye to the red kite's owner. *Maken. She almost won last year.* Chash's grip slackened on the spool and Besu faltered.

The string on their swan slipped, loosening as the red kite dove.

"It's coming for us. Pull, Grandmother!"

He grabbed the line above the spool, trying to yank it back, but he was too late.

She pulled just as the red kite sliced the air, sliding down under the swan's string. Maken yanked her spool hard and fast, snapping Besu's string in one swift motion. The spidersilk rustled in the air, teasing Chash as the wind caught it and spun it into a spiral before dropping it to the ground.

He still held the line just above the spool. It tugged at his fingers. Besu wound, then slackened the spool, trying to keep control of a kite she couldn't see. A kite that no longer flew. She had wanted to be a kite fighter so long, just to lose her battle in its first moments of flight. Chash couldn't bear it.

"You did it," he said, hoping that the sound of his voice wouldn't betray the lie. Her face was lifted, but there was no sign that she didn't believe him. She knew that the kite had fallen — she had to know — and yet, the joy on her face was so pure that Chash wanted to hold it there just a little longer.

His eyes stung as the red kite pulled away, caught by another wind. A dragon-shaped kite slammed into its middle.

One of the other kite fighters came up to them. Emi was young, but she bore the marks of a fighter already, the tip of her pinkie wrapped in bloodied cotton. Her eyes met Chash's, but she didn't say anything about the broken string in his fingers. Kites still dove and slashed through the sky overhead, circling spectators and fighters like angry eagles.

"There's about three kites above us now — can you see them?" he asked Besu.

"No." Both of her hands gripped the spool now. He moved his fingers up the line to keep the string taut and preserve the illusion that the kite still flew.

Emi furrowed her eyebrows. He mouthed, *Hush.*

"You just caught one," he said. A narrow blue diamond slashed at Norio's kite swiftly. Norio mopped his forehead with the back of his sleeve, squinting at the sky as his body hunched forward.

"It's the red kite!" Emi said. "Your bird — it just wrapped around it and yanked. And now it's falling to the ground."

A kite was falling but it wasn't red. Norio held strong despite the sweat beading on his forehead, his knuckles clenched around the handles of his spool. His red kite lifted, then neatly slit the blue diamond's string as it descended through the air. Spectators wandered toward the fighters, pointing and whispering as one kite after another fell. Emi whooped at the sky.

Chash fought the impulse to let go of the string.

"I see a blue kite," his voice wavered as Norio's aunt Lia came barreling toward the three of them. *She'll stop this — Lia has a mouth big enough to talk for three people.*

"Chash, you'll put Besu to sleep talking that way. Besu, do you remember Aso? That's his blue kite you've almost got," Lia pushed Emi out of the way to stand next to the old woman. She looked at Chash and explained, "That night your grandmother led us to the caves, Aso wouldn't go — he said we shouldn't take orders from a woman. Until a firebird spat ashes right next to him. I never saw him run so hard."

"I never liked him," Besu chuckled.

"Hold that line tight then — that wind's pulling him around like a baby bird," Lia advised. "Isn't he a little old to be out here? Kite fighters should be young if they're going to battle for the Emperor."

Chash gave her a look.

"I never knew you sewed kites, Besu. All these years and you never said a thing," Lia said. A woman Chash vaguely recognized from previous festivals had stopped to watch them. She glanced at Chash, then at Besu's hands, and smiled before waving over a cluster of elders who all looked as old as his grandmother. She pointed at Besu, saying something Chash couldn't hear.

"What was the point when I couldn't fly them?" Besu asked. "My line feels slack — what's happened?"

"The wind — it's slowing." A man picked up the story that Lia had continued. The small group that had gathered around them was growing, some faces familiar, others simply curious. Why were they all here, watching a woman with a downed kite when they could be seeing the end of the fight? How was he going to end the story before the fight did?

Chash swallowed and strengthened his grip on the cut line, yanking it up suddenly to mimic the feeling of attack.

"Chash! What's happening?" Besu called.

But before he could speak, the crowd spoke for him.

"The green is coming for you — you'd better dart to the left —"

"Besu, do you remember me from the flood in Chansec? You brought all those women from Santao and cooked for us when we were all so tired from rebuilding the houses. I still have the blanket you made for Shenshi."

"Oh, oh — I think your cords are too strong for Tado's kite — he'd best catch some wind. Besu, remember when you had to help Amna drag him home after he drank all that suls —"

"There goes the dragon! We'd better not lose you to the emperor, Besu."

The words tumbled over one another, as people from three villages competed to tell the story of Besu's kite fight, interspersing it with the memories they shared of Besu and Chash's youth. The remaining kites swooped overhead, diving and tearing at razor strings, but as each kite fell, its owner came over to weave the story of their own kite into the tale of the grandmother's conquests.

Norio was the last.

His hands were bloody, his tunic damp with sweat. Chash's heart hiccupped when the other man stopped in front of them, holding the red kite that had claimed victory. *He just came to brag.* He let go of the string. Besu began winding the spool up, then stopped as she realized there was nothing left to wind.

"Grandmother," Norio said, and Chash turned away. "Hold out your hands."

The spool dropped from her fingers as she extended her hands, palms up, to

Norio. The man knelt in the mud, gently resting the red kite on her skin.

"Our kites tangled. It was a hard fight. When our strings came together, I couldn't tell which one broke first. But mine hit the ground before yours. I honor you, Grandmother." Norio and Chash's eyes met. Chash smiled first.

"Thank you, but I cannot accept," Besu said. She patted Norio's cheek and chuckled. "I'm a bit old to join the army, don't you think?"

"Besu won! She won!" A roar came up from the crowd as a young child shouted the words, jumping up and down, caught up in the story that the village had woven. Emi grabbed Chash and wrapped her arms around his chest. He stumbled backward and hugged her back, then pulled Besu into the hug as well. Besu's answering laughter was as warm as the sun but ten times closer.

Besu shook her head at him as the three of them broke apart.

She turned to Chash. "It was a beautiful story you told me."

Her words hushed the crowd and they dispersed, people scattering across the field to pluck shreds of torn silk from the grass and collect fallen shards of glass.

"I just wanted you to win," Chash swallowed, his throat dry. A great wave of emotion welled up inside of him for this woman who had made him what he was. And he wasn't a warrior.

"Your heart is kind, but I worry that I've failed you." Besu sighed. "You didn't have to lie. I wasn't smiling because I was winning. I was just happy to share your dream. I should never have asked you to give that up."

He reached for her hands and took them in his. Her fingers matched his own, with knuckles a little too big for her hands, and curved, even nails. *These hands and everything they've taught me... this is who I am. Who I want to be. That man doesn't need a war to be proud.*

"The village loves you, Grandmother. I love you," he said. "The emperor has enough men to fight for him. Maybe it's time more of us became tailors."

"If I had someone to help with the dresses, I might be able to sew a kite once in a while," Besu leaned against him as they walked through the field of battered kites. "Teach you a few things about flying them."

"What? Train your competitor?"

Besu swatted at him, and they laughed. Chash thought of the days that lay ahead of them both — of saying goodbye to the work that he hated and devoting himself to pattern, color, and thread.

Since we don't have wings, we make kites. His grandmother's words came back to him and Chash smiled. There was more than one way to fly.

See Gwen Whiting's story "Since We Don't Have Wings" online at Metaphorosis.
If you liked it, leave a comment. Authors love that!
Remember to subscribe to our e-mail updates so you'll know when new stories are posted.

About the story

The world and ideas of "Since We Don't Have Wings" have their origins in a few different places. As I was writing early drafts of this piece during the pandemic, I was part of a roleplaying group that had started using the Ryuutama system. If you've never played the game, the best description of it I've heard is "Miyazaki meets Oregon Trail". Though "Wings" isn't really connected to that campaign or characters, the game inspired me to think about fantasy on a small scale.

Much of the fantasy I grew up with focuses on a singular hero or sometimes group of heroes going on long journeys to do heroic things. What does heroism look like when you never leave your home?

I've also been fortunate to have been raised by and around generations of strong women and with men who support those women. For much of my life, however, people outside the family have questioned and sometimes challenged that dynamic because various individuals didn't follow gender "norms". Chash was chosen as the protagonist of this story as a way of rejecting the idea both of the "hero" and because I wanted to show that growing into manhood doesn't have to look like going to war or proving one's self through physical action. Sometimes, the heroes are the ones who stay. This is a theme that's also reflected in Besu, his grandmother, but it takes a different form because her choices (or perhaps, lack of) were different.

A question for the author

Q: What is the hardest part of writing for you?

A: The hardest part of writing for me is often knowing when to stop. It's very easy to get caught up, not only when writing in the world that I've created, but also when building the world itself. I enjoy research more than I probably should, and often look around at ideas, events, and people of the past when brainstorming short stories. It interests me to take what was and instead imagine what could have been.

About the author

A lifelong Pacific Northwesterner, Gwen Whiting spends her days working at museums and her evenings scribbling out one story or another. When Gwen isn't writing or working, she's spending time with her family, reading a book, or dabbling in activities inspired by whatever project she's working on. She's tried everything from belly dance to basket weaving and is currently researching beekeeping.

gwen-whiting.com, @Gwen_Whiting

Time, Wolf, Emit, Flow

Anna Madden

Time watched a dust storm approaching fast. At her side, Wolf whined, and she stroked his moss-green fur to calm her own worries as much as his.

The rest of the pack darted for cover, their movements blurs of sage and evergreen. Younger packmates reshaped their inner light into different forms, including wolves, but also hare and elk and coyote. Age brought attachment, a fear of change—a rigidity. Time wore the strangest form of all: two-legged, covered by a gown of pale lichen, a leafy mane falling midway down her back. It was a form that had once belonged to the

Shapers alone. Wolf complained at her choice, though he curled into Time's side readily enough each eve to warm her almost furless hide.

The sky darkened. The pack's territory was no longer blessed by the light of the Shapers, the winds death-still. Dust fell from leaden clouds overhead and collected atop the plains. The hoary flakes smoldered near flats of obsidian rock bed. Fragile switchglass—with its crystal-like leaves—grew between the cracks. As dust accumulated to a thick powder, the land turned the color of aged muzzles, the ground opaque and ugly.

"It's useless," Time said to Wolf. "We'll never finish the wind-maker."

"Don't say that," Wolf said, his voice husky. "Your design can be replicated, used to stir the winds and open the Light Gate. The Shapers' light will return. We'll survive this lean season, same as others."

Time stood still. She knew Wolf spoke in dreams rather than full truths. He didn't smell the wounds she carried. Time dwelled on the pack's losses, and the transience from green to gray across the land. She prided herself on her mind, her focus, but lately the collecting dust felt suffocating, desolation piling like leaf litter and unanswered questions.

The pack's dependence on the Shapers had made them weak. There was too much the pack had never been told or taught. The dust storms were worse and worse. The Shapers had kept the dust from accumulating, but they'd left, abandoning this world to a never-ending season of neglect.

Time's back ached, strained from gathering metals and broken glass to be ready before the storm hit. Dust flurried. It stung her eyes and scratched her ever-dry throat.

Wolf dug through a pile of hard-found supplies taken from the mountains' feet and the plains beyond, then picked up a piece of copper in his jaw.

Watching him, Time wiped a film of dust from her eyes. Her sight didn't thank her, only picking up more grit. Time thought of better days, of racing after Wolf, of clean air and laughter and unappreciated sunshine. She didn't run anymore. With the horrid dust in her lungs, polluting her light, she'd wilted.

Time coughed and surveyed her work area. It was a mess, exposed, set on the eastern side of the dust-covered steppes where the Light Gate stood like a dead thing. It was an entrance to the river of light, its currents unknown.

The gate was ancient. It had been built by the Shapers, made of metal and glass, as forbidding as the dusk and ungiving as winter.

Around it, there were piles of sorted copper, zinc, and tin. There were sheets of broken glass and a jar of clear flux, mixed by her own hand, used to clean the metal before soldering it. The building materials of the Shapers. Time dared to build as they had, so the pack avoided her, their gazes splintered with distrust.

All but Wolf.

Something poked her shoulder. She glanced over. Wolf had jabbed her with the copper gripped in his muzzle. His fur was bright green, the ends sparkling like dew on fern leaves. She took the metal from him and debated on its placement, trying one spot, then another. Her dull, tired fingers worked the copper around the edges of a large glass shard. It stood on its side, propped with a bit of spare metalwork next to the wind-maker's frame, angled to catch the sun. She had constructed it near the Light Gate so the wind it made could unlock the currents the Shapers had left before they closed the way behind them.

"No more copper," Time said before Wolf grabbed another piece between his sharp teeth. "We have enough to solder the blades and the tail. After, we'll attach the base." She coughed again.

"You'll finish it," Wolf said, his voice forced brightness, his tail wagging. "I know you will."

Time looked at the Light Gate and imagined all the answers it might provide, once opened. She tried to be like Wolf. She tried to hope.

Three days later, the storm ruled, and dust piled higher. It wasn't an optimal condition for work, but Time wouldn't risk waiting. The rest of their packmates hid in what cover they could find, braving the open at midday to hunt light while Time continued the work.

Youths had started wearing the forms of nomadic grazers. Cattle and horse and caribou—with muzzles, strong hooves, horns, and thick fur—better to trek through the banks of unstable, layered dust. To graze the muted switchglass struggling to grow despite it.

A scatter of hoofprints circled the supply piles. Scavengers had approached the Light Gate itself, touching its dusty edges with paw and snout.

The sun was shrouded by a thick gray veil. Time finished the placements and started soldering. The metals were bonding well. Wolf kept close to her elbow, wiping dust away with a flux-covered paw. Time held her soldering iron with expertise.

The next glass shard was in easy reach, resting atop the wind-maker's frame. As she adjusted the next joint, she foolishly leaned too far. Her knees pressed against the loose piece. The glass wavered, then tipped downward.

"Wolf, grab it quick!"

He snapped at it, his teeth grazing the too-smooth surface, but the piece fell, its weight carrying it down. It shattered, the pieces ricocheting against the wind-maker's skeleton.

Time eyed her supply pile, but the remaining glass shards she'd gathered with Wolf were needed as suncatchers to power the wind-maker. How could she have been so stupid? She squeezed her eyes shut.

"I'll go," Wolf said, stretching his front legs. "There's some to the north, I think, where we've hunted before." She opened her mouth, about to tell him she would go too, but then he growled softly. "You stay," he said. "Save your strength."

She almost argued, but the words forming on her tongue belonged to a Shaper, arrogant, dipped in greater knowledge—or the appearance of it.

Looking down, Time sighed. "I'll clean up this mess."

When Wolf returned, he dragged a heavy glass shard as perfect as the first, but it had claimed something in return. He shook his fur, which had lost its shine, and she could make out light-seeping cuts upon his paws. He panted, his tongue hanging out of his mouth. She thanked the Shapers' light he wasn't hurt worse, but her eyes watered when she heard him muffle a cough, pressing his muzzle into his fur-clad chest.

What would she do without him, if he faded, lacking the strength to continue?

Time jerked a hand through her leafy hair and cleared her throat. She rearranged her collection of metals. "Let's get back to work."

With the second attempt, she didn't rush. She built extra supports for the wind-maker, then Wolf helped her lift the replacement shard into place. He braced it while she soldered the glass to the frame before attaching the blades and the tail. When Time was certain nothing would fall off or shatter, she squared her shoulders and joined the final seams with solder.

They set up their array of suncatchers next.

The angles of their light brightened a patch of tall switchglass despite its buried roots, returning treasured hues of olive and sage. Time tried not to cough as she directed Wolf, whose deft paws tilted each glass piece a different angle to best capture the sunlight. When they had finished, Time and Wolf pushed the wind-maker onto four silver feet.

"Turn it, a hair more to the left," Time said, motioning impatiently, eager. She had started to let herself hope this might work. "Be careful. It's not quite level, and if it falls—" She swallowed. "We'll adjust the suncatchers as needed afterward."

Wolf groaned, his back taut, his strong jaw clamped over metal and glass in an awkward bite. He tugged hard, his claws cutting lines into the dust beneath him. The wind-maker's base creaked as it pivoted. Wolf tended the suncatchers again, nudging them with his nose while Time wheezed into the inside of her elbow.

She steadied herself against the wind-maker. Its metal had a mirror-like quality, capturing her dull likeness. In memory, her complexion was bright, as vivid as new spring stems.

Time shook her hair back. It rustled dryly to her ankles. "I look awful."

Wolf nuzzled her knees. Once, he'd have agreed with her, and tried to persuade her to try another form. "The wind-maker will work," he said instead.

Time eyed Wolf, long-limbed, his ears cupped in her direction, and fur still dappled by light despite his developing cough. Sometimes, she wondered at his forbearance, at his willingness to aid her. Wolf had stopped hunting with the pack because of her. He said it was his choice, the same as hers to wear the form of a Shaper. Even now, he offered her a toothy smile.

She doubted him. What did he see in her? A faded thing. A memory of light, her remaining days as fragile and thin as withering switchglass. Time dipped her chin.

"Look!" Wolf said, his ears swiveling toward the wind-maker's blades. His light flared moss-bright within his fur. "It's working."

Time watched the wind-maker. The suncatchers fed it steady light, and the blades turned, slowly at first but then faster. The wind stirred, waking seeded secrets, finishing the sequence implemented in all Shaper builds.

The Light Gate glowed, faint at first, widening, flickering; the blink of a great yellow eye. Its opening revealed the river of light: its flow the radiance of the dawn, the warmth of high summer. Its brilliance glinted off the wind-maker. Dust sparkled.

Time stepped closer to the Light Gate, enchanted by its gilded beauty, its bright currents.

Too late, she realized its danger. Her thoughts shifted from a soft glow of wonder to a searing fear of something powerful and unknowable.

The Light Gate seemed to breathe in, hot, arid, tasting of burning hair. Her inner light crackled from between her lips, her skin. She struggled to step back even as the river of light pulled her in. A withered leaf plucked from the stem, falling.

"Wolf!" Time cried.

She thought she heard him howl back.

Was this death, then? Time panicked. She wasn't ready to die. She wanted to feel the sun's true warmth, and to run fast beside Wolf once more. She wasn't ready. She wasn't finished with her work yet.

The sky disappeared. In its place there was the too-bright light of the river. Wings flapped high above. She heard them above the gold-flecked river. As unformed as mist, barely outlined, with lace-like plumes. Feathers grazed Time's right cheek, then flapped away.

The air cooled, misty and salt-licked, and the sky returned.

It was the wrong color.

"Emit, is that you? Emit?"

Time stirred. A light hovered near her. Blurry-eyed, she couldn't make out the familiar shape of Wolf. Time blinked, then blinked again. There were no greens to comfort her, nor grays to worry over.

"Everything's the wrong color," Time mumbled, rubbing her eyes. As she took a breath, she realized her throat was clear, the air refreshed, the sky dust-free. She stood quickly. A swelling, rippling sea surged at her feet. Edges of metal and glass rose from the water. The shapes weren't natural, but sculpted. It couldn't be, but it had to be: the Light Gate.

It was in ruin, half-claimed by deep waters.

Time bit her bottom lip to stop from crying out in defeat. She remembered the wind-maker clearly, and the burning air as she fell into the river of light. But the pain had washed away. This didn't feel like death. There was too much fear in her heart for this to be the end.

Time was uncertain of all but Wolf's loss at her side, the realization worse than any number of dust storms. The wind-maker had been intended to coax the winds back, to open the Light Gate and return the light of the Shapers to the pack's territory, and maybe, hope against hope, to clear the dust storms for good.

Opening the Light Gate hadn't been meant to send her elsewhere, far from

Wolf, their pack, their shared joys and despairs.

Something rubbery pecked at her fingertips.

"Emit?" the same stranger's voice asked, calling her that backward name again. "Why did you change your light into these?"

Time sat up and looked at her palms, trying to center herself by focusing on something familiar in a world reshaped. "I—my name is Time. I prefer having hands so I can build things."

As she spoke, Time looked up and met two jewel-like eyes, their brilliant and unexpected shade reminding her she wasn't alone. This wasn't a Shaper, but not a packmate either. "Who are you?" she asked.

"What a funny joke," the stranger with beautiful eyes said, a playfulness in his tone. "I am Flow, of course." His chosen form was a dolphin. A streamlined body with a round head and a tall dorsal fin.

Flow blew water from his blowhole, then broke into song:

> *Mountains gleam silver,*
> *the sky drips of gold honey,*
> *but none are my blue.*

Time looked at his flippers and tilted her head. Flow opened his beak wider, smiling brightly, though imperfectly— crookedly. Wolf smiled like that. Time was heartened by the echoed expression of it. Flow turned and splashed her with his tail fluke. He flickered into the form of a bright-scaled fish, then back to a dolphin.

"Come on, Emit. Let's test out this ugly new form of yours. Race you to the next wave! Loser eats a mouthful of bubbles."

Time pushed aside thoughts of Wolf, burying the guilt and the panic, centering herself in the calm of analyzing a problem. A cold focus that pushed away emotion. Like a dream, this place felt unreal, and perhaps that made its unusualness less frightening.

What had happened? The logical part of her said she'd done as she'd meant: opening the Light Gate, but then she'd fallen into the river of light, its currents bringing her into unknown territory. A journey which in theory, she might reverse.

But who was Emit? Why wasn't Flow's friend on this side of the gate? A mystery with complexities that forced Time to realize the truth: she was no Shaper. The cracks in her focus splintered, and despair sent a chill down her spine.

She was nothing.

No better than a speck of dust for all her grasping to be more.

Time wanted desperately to run, to put as much distance between herself and her failings as possible. She sprang forward, her light-filled feet keeping atop the water's surface. It felt like she was in control as she tried to escape.

And she had not run in a very long time.

The urge to flee took over reason and purpose, primal and wild.

Time wasn't sure where she had come to, but the sea was beautiful, full of happier memories than the pack's dusty plains. Its waves were untiring and graceful, and the winds overhead didn't sputter or sigh. If Wolf were beside her, she thought, all would be well.

And there it was: the heartache. The despair. The emptiness that could not be filled, nor outrun no matter how light-strong she might have become.

Time followed closely behind Flow's tail fluke. Like Wolf, he was faster than her. If he got too far ahead, she'd have no one.

She'd be completely, totally alone.

"Slow down," she cried out, though when she tried harder, her light-strong legs moved atop the seawater almost as swiftly as his fins within it. "Please. Where are we going?"

Flow slowed, letting her draw abreast to his dorsal fin. He splashed her with a wave. "To the Crack, Emit. Where else?"

As they traveled, Flow sang to her of blue things. There were sapphires, asters, indigo dye, and blueberries. There were morpho butterflies, jays, and bluebells. Time could not keep track of them all, nor did she want to, for it was only a reminder of how little she understood.

"So many," Time said in bitterness, her breaths deep, her calves burning. "I've never heard of some."

Flow laughed, the sound a bubbling spring, his smile open and sweet. "I love to play games with you."

"You talk like we're old friends."

He looked over at her with a hurt expression. "Aren't we?"

Time swallowed back frustration, though she longed to tell him he knew nothing of her: that he was too carefree, that Emit was gone, lost. He should be worried.

But if she told him that, wouldn't she only offer him pain? Perhaps it was better to be ignorant. To be unaware.

She caught her reflection in the water. Her long hair parted to the opposite side from her usual style. Still, she looked like herself, only mirrored. And she brimmed with light. Her skin reflected the sea's brilliant blue.

She remembered a winged form in the passage of the Light Gate, bringing a frown to her lips. Had it been a Shaper she'd seen? Was Emit one? Perhaps if she could find a Shaper, this mess would have a solution.

Looking around, Time hunted for signs of the Shapers. She had questions, and there were answers to be found in this place, surely.

They reached what Flow called the Crack.

Time's feet splashed to a halt. She almost wept, for the sea had been parted like an unhealed wound, and the water fell into its trap. A waterfall carried the sea down and away. Had this place been broken by the Shapers' absence too?

Strangers wearing forms of tarpon and sailfish and gannets had gathered around it, playing within the frothy waters, jumping and flying along its girth. These kin of Flow's weren't Shapers.

The sea floor looked the same dark shade of obsidian as the plains of her home, where the pack's territory stretched. Strong rock, not easily injured. One hand kept flying strands of hair out of Time's mouth. It was no longer green or leafy. It streamed across her face, its roots damp.

She stepped forward. "I could fix this. The two halves can be brought together and sealed. I'd need materials, metal to solder together, but then the water wouldn't run off like this."

Flow snorted. "Water is not meant to stay in one place. It would feel trapped if it did."

"I—" Time didn't understand. Wouldn't the sea drain away, eventually? Flow seemed untroubled.

Time exhaled. The Shapers weren't here, their scent trail nonexistent. She pictured her wind-maker. It had proven itself as dangerous as her own curiosity. Should she leave things be for once, for fear of making them worse? Maybe Wolf was glad she wasn't around anymore, making messes. Breaking things. Maybe he had rejoined their pack with glee. Her shoulders dipped.

"You've never been a worrier, Emit," Flow said. "Nothing is whole in this world. Life needs a flaw or two."

"I see," she said, but she didn't.

They slept apart. Time curled up on the shore, while Flow floated in gentle waves. The quiet and the doubts that grew stronger in the dark made her heartsick for Wolf unbearable. She tossed and turned, fighting off nightmares. When Time woke, there was a horrible storm raging overhead. Dust flakes sunk into the sea's waters, polluting it.

"No, no," Time cried, trying to scoop bits out with her hands. "Not here too."

A gentle fin touched her left ankle. "What's wrong, Emit?"

Time pointed to the troubled sky. "A storm's here. The dust is already falling."

Flow whistled, then exhaled through his blowhole. "The dust will wash away, as it always does." He swam, circling her. "The Crack will filter it, for the sea carries such impurities there."

"But, the dust..." Time considered trying to explain it all. To convince him she wasn't Emit. To tell Flow of the river of light, her anger at the Shapers. Her fear of never seeing Wolf again. Her hope that she could build as well as the Shapers. Of Wolf and his moss-green fur and the switchglass of the plains.

Maybe the answer was admitting she didn't know what it all meant. That this world was flawed and always would bear the scars of what had come before. She had dabbled in a power she didn't understand, and she'd taken Emit from Flow without even knowing she had the power to do so. There could be no other explanation than that Emit's disappearance correlated with Time's appearance.

The Shapers had left great hardship in their absence. Maybe it was unfair to think they were meant to be perfect, unflawed. Their kind had never held all the answers, and the pack was no different.

Time had thought she could give the world a form she'd shaped—that followed her own rules. She'd lost something of herself by trying to control so much. There was focus in her, and discipline, but she'd lost a spark for life itself, always trying to go back to a season that no longer existed.

Time shook her head. "The Crack isn't a flaw, is it?"

Flow laughed. "You finally see!"

She looked at Flow but only saw Wolf before her, his ears drooped, his light almost spent.

"Shapers guide me," Time said. "There's something I must build, and I'll need your help."

They traveled fast, catching the sun at the Crack. Time tried to explained as best she could about the plains, Wolf, that she knew the chosen form of Emit was a winged one. Flow played along, thinking it all a great game.

Time searched for materials, sometimes catching sight of Flow leaping clear from the water, then flying as a seagull. She noted how the dirty water collected and spilled over the waterfall.

Time dove below the sea's surface and found two treasures. The first was a smooth piece of shell-like glass, quite elegant, slightly dished from the water's touch. The second piece was jagged and sharp.

At her request, they traveled west next, approaching familiar silver peaks which tilted the wrong direction. More and more, this world seemed a reflection of her own. Wolf and Flow, so similar, yet different. Time and Emit, two halves of an unseeable whole.

Did the river of light connect them all, a path between worlds built by the Shapers' hands?

Her mind was lost in a puzzle she'd never solve, and it was easiest to tackle the hardest questions. It pushed aside doubts and confusion. She prioritized thought over heart. Questions consumed her. If there was a Crack in the sea, what was its sibling on the plains? Why was the Light Gate whole in her land, but in ruin within the sea?

Busy hands kept away the loss of Wolf. She used the jagged glass to free zinc, lead, and copper and took her findings to the site of the drowned Light Gate, and began to build a mirror, for she needed a way to reshape what had been worn away.

She needed to remind the gate of its unbroken form by bringing together its pieces, bathed in light. Then she had to convince it to open. She'd used wind to wake the first Light Gate, but should she trust her instincts and try water here instead?

At first, she tried to replicate old techniques, but the bowl-shaped glass was not like her wind-maker's design, nor did she have so skilled a helper as Wolf at her side. The materials wouldn't cooperate without proper tools either. Instead, Time let the glass keep its curved shape and added a thin splinter of the old Light Gate as a stem below it. Flow enjoyed the novelty of it all. He helped her as he could, changing to a pelican, scooping up mouthfuls of saltwater to empty into the basin-like shell.

When the mirror was done, it caught the sunset's rays, dazzling Time's eyes.

Time peeked into that brilliance and saw a glint of green, then gray. It showed her what she sought: a likeness of her truest self, and behind it, dust-smothered plains, more dust falling still. She felt the mirror's edges in her hand's grip, and looked deeply, hungrily. The plains of home spread out before her in the water's reflection. She could see them, hear them.

Wind whistled through switchglass, making it chime. There were scents of fur and dusty sunlight. The wind-maker still spun, and the suncatchers remained in place, their bright rays spotlighting the metal framework. The Light Gate was open, a stream like a vein of gold flowing out, finding a path through rocks, the plains, renewing the land with the Shapers' light. The ground was covered in broken shards, and Wolf was curled up among them, his tail wrapped over his light-bleeding paws. His muzzle had burn marks.

He looked dim. But he wasn't alone.

Another form circled in the air, the outline of wings forming a bruised shadow below. Time had never seen a form that didn't shine. All but invisible, Emit's light held the barest suggestion of form. She twirled, then swooped. Her wings created wind of their own. Though she didn't glow, nor flare, she was faster, fiercer, than anyone Time had ever met.

But light was nothing without control.

Emit flew erratically. She circled over and over in the air. Wolf observed from the ground and whined softly.

In defeat, Emit landed near him, the weak outline of her head tilted to the side as though she listened closely, his breathing guiding her. Her eyes were opaque and clouded, as though they'd been burned away from within. She folded her beautiful, hazy wings against her sides. "Are you toying with me," she asked, angry, "saying the gate is one direction when it's really another?"

Wolf growled. "Keep back."

"You're all bite, no bark," Emit said, her voice yet a raging storm.

"I told you where to fly," Wolf said. "I didn't lie. It's you who can't find the way."

"All I see are shadows and the faintest of shades," Emit said. "This strange place —I can't navigate it. And you—you're no better, bleeding light as you are, with that tail held between your legs."

"I'm waiting for Time," Wolf said, a cough following his words, before his lips peeled back again to show his teeth.

Glints of long plumes shone as Emit shifted closer. "I didn't choose to come here. These gates were meant to die. Rusted traps left by the Shapers to catch us in their ugly teeth."

Wolf's growl turned into a snarl. "The Shapers did not set traps."

"They were hunters, same as you," Emit said.

"Time doesn't think so," Wolf said, lowering his hackles, smiling crookedly.

"You'll see. She'll find them, before she returns."

"You remind me of someone, under your fangs," Emit said, doubt edging her voice. "He's probably having too much fun to even notice I'm gone."

Wolf wagged his tail, weakly. "Trust me, no one could ever forget you."

Time stepped back from the mirror and wiped wet eyes. The sky wasn't at full light. She shouldn't lean too close or look too deeply into the mirror's center until all was ready.

Wolf was waiting for her, but if Time left now, Emit wouldn't find her way back. She hadn't asked to be torn from her blue world.

Emit needed a glimpse of something blue, a beacon, to guide her flight home. Time turned her back on the mirror and stepped back into the sea.

Yawning, his beak held comically wide, Flow swam around Time in gentle circles. He flattened his light into triangular pectoral fins, becoming a sleek and graceful manta ray.

"When I look into the mirror again," Time said, "I may not be as I have been of late. I may change."

Flow flicked water at her with his tail when he saw her frown. "I can't get used to that form on you anyway."

"You're one to talk," Time said. "I've never known another to change forms so often as you."

He laughed. "Everyone seems so set on picking a specific one. I can't understand it."

Time dipped below the surface and found a round blue rock the same shade as Flow's jeweled eyes.

Flow slept. Time drifted away in the night, then raced back to her mirror, her heels kicking up water. She hoped to catch the dawn in its basin without Flow's company, for she didn't want to risk him following her.

Time reached her mirror at the site of the Light Gate's ruin. Taking her blue rock, holding it tight, she put her hands over the mirror's rim. She looked into its calm surface where she saw the opposite bank.

"Emit," Time said, her voice rippling the pooled water, "I'm going to try sending you some blue to guide your flight home."

Time dropped the blue rock into the mirror's waters and hoped this gate she'd built would do as planned, creating a ford between both worlds. Holding her breath, she watched the rock skip across the surface of the river of light, carrying the color of the sea to the plains.

It had worked.

She heard a flap of wings. Before fear overtook or reason out-won against what her heart was telling her, Time plunged her face into the mirror's cool waters and fell into the river of light.

The air burned, bright as fire. It stole the light from Time's lips, her hands, her very breath.

Twice as painful as the first time.

She could feel it tearing at her inner light, hungry for it, unmaking her form.

Above, Emit flew, given away by beating wings and the glint of light off her delicate outline.

Time let the currents take her, surrendering to their pull, her world searing, a storm of blinding light. She closed her eyes. One fading leaf floating atop the river of light.

Switchglass chimed, softly. There were scents of musk, of mud, of heated rock. Time opened her eyes to familiar green eyes and a burned muzzle. A wolfish grin, just a tad crooked. His breath was uneven, labored.

"I thought I'd lost you, Time."

"There's still a bit of me left," Time said, her voice weak, raspy. Her hands were cold and numb. Escaped light dissipated into tiny white flames dying around her.

She was a stem with no leaves left to pull free. She looked at Wolf at her side, and yet so far away, drifting further with each shattered breath she gulped down. Long ago, she'd tried other forms, but never that of a wolf. And why not? She'd worn so many others, when she hadn't let the fear of change ripen within.

What she had done once, she could do again.

Slowly, she reached for her inner light, unraveling her already damaged form, matching her breaths to Wolf's.

He crawled closer, his ears flattened against his head, his cracked skin bleeding thin trails of light.

"The pack needs to learn how to tend the wind-maker," Time said. "Its blades will blow the dust through the Light Gate. There is a blue sea on the other side. It will filter it. The glass plains will be wiped green once more. The pack will hunt together again. All will be as it was."

"Why are you telling me all this?" Wolf said, fear a wet rasp in his throat. "Without you, it can never be as it was."

The dawn broke free of the gray clouds. The sun's brightness poured in, bringing hues of green together. The sunlight glistened against the metal of the wind-maker, the profile of the Light Gate.

Time felt her form fall apart. She let it. Her light flowed out in a new current, molding to another shape, falling beneath moss-green fur. It refilled what had seeped from cuts like dripping sap. She knew now what she had always known: their bond was a strength that shone through all other light. More than anything, she wanted Wolf to run across plains once more, through fields of shining switchglass.

She thought of Emit, flying overhead, her inner light bright and true.

Wolf's breaths steadied.

She blinked and looked at the world through Wolf's eyes. The plains rose before her, their collected dust, and the silvery mountains she knew and loved. She felt the air stir against her fur, felt the happiness of her wagging tail, heard herself pant.

I'm here, with you, Time thought to Wolf. *Our light is joined, the dust we'd breathed in shed like an undercoat. Let's make brighter days than these. Promise me.*

Wolf howled. His paws were whole again, the inner light within renewing what had wilted. He pounced forward with his snout pointed the direction of their favorite meadow. His joy was hers. Her days were his. They ran together, as one. Her love for him an eternal memory of light, undimmed.

See Anna Madden's story "Time, Wolf, Emit, Flow" online at Metaphorosis.
If you liked it, leave a comment. Authors love that!
Remember to subscribe to our e-mail updates so you'll know when new stories are posted.

About the story

I make stained glass, and I wanted to capture the magic of that craft in this tale. Glass, light, colors, reflections, and metal brought together. I imagined a rippled blue piece of glass soldered to a leafy green one. Dust can accumulate on glass, dulling its brilliance, so why not have it be the same in this world? And what if beings formed of light existed in this strange realm? What would they look like? These are questions I'd ponder while making suncatchers, cutting glass and arranging it.

I especially adore worldbuilding that feels like something completely of its own, set apart, with an atmosphere that cloaks the reader and inspires imagery of a place unlike anywhere else. When I read stories, I don't often want all the answers to a world's origin or to have every rule explained to me, but a balance is needed nonetheless. This particular story of mine is one that took some effort to find that line. When I stumbled upon the Shapers, that helped a great deal in filling in pieces of necessary lore, but their history is still ancient and shrouded in the unknown.

The heart of this story is Wolf and Time's relationship, though. I love fiction centered on strong friendships, and I've always been fascinated with the idea of befriending a wolf—a connection to something wild and untamable, fierce but beautiful.

A question for the author

Q: Do you prefer your SFF as books or movies?

A: SFF books take me on an internal journey that movies can't often replicate. Written works are fluid, with rich details that I can sow and feed with my own imagination. I crave stories that seem to breathe as they unfold, becoming uniquely mine as I consume them. In *All the Murmuring Bones* by A. G. Slatter, I loved exploring that dark, secret-laden world through Miren's eyes, seeing her thoughts and perspective so intimately. But I certainly enjoy SFF movies, the talents of many creating a few hours of magic. *Dune* blew me away last year even though I knew the story already. I enjoyed the insect-like ornithopters and seeing those colossal sandworms, and I've re-listened to the soundtrack often while writing. Perhaps I should retry answering this question and say SFF books are like strawberry ice cream to me, but that doesn't mean I won't eat mint chocolate chip if it's offered.

About the author

Anna Madden lives in Fort Worth, Texas. She has an English degree from the University of Missouri— Kansas City. In free time she gardens, mountain bikes, and makes stained glass.

www.annamadden.com, @anna_madden_

Her Spirit Animal

L.A.W. Butler

Atynleigh leaned into the wind as she pulled her wool shawl closer around her face. The freezing wind was part of her daily trek along the shores of the great lake, yet someone had to check on the well-being of the creature that lived on the high point above the cove. In Atynleigh's small, damaged family, that someone meant her. The creature must be attended to, and Atynleigh was a dutiful child. So, she shrugged the pack on her back into a more comfortable position and trudged on.

Far above the cove the dull sun added a meager warmth to the dark slate that formed a grassless apron in front of the hut where the creature lived. This morning he had painfully made his way to a high stump of stone that separated the path from the lake cliff and was resting in the sun. His eyes wandered to the restless, gray waters of the great lake below him. Sometimes he looked, and with some regard, to the low mountains and thick forest that lay to the east and south, and to the steeper valley with its swift, narrow river that formed the western lands. But the lake, stretched across the northern horizon, was his home, and it was this that he longed for.

Knowing that the girl would surely come that day, the man—if man he was—had clumsily stoked a fire for tea. He knew the child would be cold and he knew the burden he placed on the family in the valley.

The sun was the width of an outstretched hand above the horizon when Atynleigh approached the hut. She called to the creature as she approached the cabin.

"I am here," she heard in response.

She knew it was difficult for Creature to speak aloud. His voice came in a wet, soft whisper. Yet, she had heard the words of his greeting clearly, with its strange, precise accent. At such times she knew he had been thinking the words. When Creature used his mind instead of his throat, his words came easily. She also knew that he could hear her thoughts. But just as it was easier for him to speak with his mind, it was easier for her to speak with her throat, and this was how they communicated.

Atynleigh remembered when she and her mother had found—rescued, saved—the creature from death on the stone beach some distance from their home. He had been injured and in pain from a fearsome wound on his side.

She and Mother had been fishing far down the cove. Fish had been sparse for weeks and they had followed signs of schooling fish past the safety of the harbor. Mother was a skilled fisherman, from a long line of men and women who had made their living on the lake's water. Atynleigh's mother and father had enjoyed fishing together, but Father had died months ago and now Atynleigh was Mother's fishing companion.

They had entered a shallow cove where a rippling surface spoke of an abundance of fish. They were about to toss their net when Atynleigh stayed her mother's strong arm and nodded noiselessly toward the near shore. A man appeared to be crawling across the beach, not even crawling so much as moving his limbs in response to unremitting pain. All of this, as well as something undefinable about his dark, rough appearance, made mother and daughter hesitate as they scanned the shoreline for danger. These were unsettled times. Even aiding the obviously sick or wounded required a serious decision.

"We need to get closer," Atynleigh whispered.

Mother nodded. They were both thinking the same thing. If someone had been on this shore to help Father, he might have lived instead of bleeding out in frigid water, alone and without hope. On that fateful day, rising waves from a sudden storm had thrown Father, as skilled a man as there was in a small boat, into the shallows. He would have survived with only bruises, but he had crashed down on a broken iron hoop from a submerged and rotten barrel. The metal drove deep into his thigh, cutting the femoral artery. Without help, he had never stood a chance.

That loss gave both mother and daughter courage to offer this stranger the lifeline which had been denied Atynleigh's father. Still, they approached cautiously. Mother slid from the boat as it hissed against the pebbles and grounded itself on the shore. Atynleigh, with her sharp eyes, would watch the tree line for possible danger. They did not need to discuss these arrangements, they simply knew.

The man had rolled on his back and looked in their direction. He had clearly been aware of their approach. Now, he neither moved nor made a sound. He lay a short ten yards from shore, his head toward them with golden eyes watching their every move.

"Do good."

"What?" her mother asked.

"I said nothing," Atynleigh replied, looking at her mother for the first time since the boat came to its stop. "I thought you told me..."

They both looked toward the man with his pleading eyes. They were sure he had made no sound, but they knew what they had heard. Atynleigh impulsively joined her mother in the water as they ran together—to do good.

They needed the strength of their desire to do the right thing, for as they approached the injured man, they saw that it was, in fact, no man at all.

"A Spirit Animal," Mother whispered, stopping short some distance from the creature. She had hesitated as she said this and both Mother and Atynleigh looked at each other and then back to the creature. Spirit animals were known to exist in this lake, sometimes seen, sometimes feared, sometimes revered in a way just short of worship. The Spirit Animals were creatures of legend and song. They were neither man nor beast, but part of both worlds and it is said that they could talk to both the fish and the fishermen. Many a person who had disappeared was said to have been called to the lake by a Spirit Animal, never to be seen again. There were others who said they would have been lost except for a Spirit Animal that guided (or carried) them to a safe shore after a storm or accident.

Atynleigh shook with fear and awe; this was certainly the creature of the legends. What lay before them had the configuration of a man, but the scales and gills of a fish. He had a muscular tail and spiked dorsal fins down his back like a lizard. His face was reptilian. The eyes were golden, large, and bulging, with pupils constricted in pain. Down the creature's side, from armpit to hip, a bloody slice had been opened by some sharp object.

The creature looked at them again and they heard more thoughts, but of garbled and uncertain meaning. The creature was able to capture feelings more than specific words, though sometimes one emerged as the other.

"Spirit Animal," was suddenly repeated back to them, and then, softer, the repeated plea, "…do good."

Atynleigh had looked to her mother, fearful, wondering what they should do. Mother's worried eyes moved from her daughter to the creature and then her shivering lips closed in a look of decision and determination. Mother hurried back to the boat, caught up the net and ran back to her daughter.

"We will spread this beside the creature, lift him on to it as best we can and ferry him back to the cabin. I can care for the wound there."

They went to work but heard no more from the creature save a feeling of intense pain when they moved him.

He was still alive when they brought him to their cabin.

From the early days of Creature's recovery, even those perilous first days lying on a pallet by the fire in their cabin, Atynleigh had noticed his golden eyes following everything she and Mother did. He tried to understand their thoughts and share his with them, but communication was halting and incomplete. Creature had watched as they spent the long, cold nights working, working, working, until the brief hour before exhaustion sent them to bed. Once they called the day's work enough, she and Mother would pull out the chess board and play a fast, deadly game.

Their game of chess was not the slow, studied game of deep thinkers. Theirs was like their lives, a series of quick decisions.

Mother and Father had played chess. They had taught Atynleigh while she was still sitting on their knees and as she grew older, that any one of that trio might win on any given night. Their board was simply functional, but the pieces—ah, those chessmen. Father had carved them from walrus tusks. They were tiny because tusk was a precious commodity. But the carving was fine and animated, with carefully detailed faces.

The creature had quickly become fascinated with the nightly chess match.

Two days after Creature came to the cabin he was starting to move painfully and slowly. Each time he reopened his wound, but the bleeding was less each time. He ate hungrily. That would have been a problem, except that fish had started coming to the cove. The first day a mass of mussels had apparently thrown themselves onto the shore by the cabin, enough to fill a bucket. It had turned into a feast for all of them.

By the fourth day Creature had been lucid enough to ask what this 'chess' was. A full week later Creature hobbled toward the chess board and began observing the game. He watched, trying simple questions using his soft, bubbling voice, or speaking directly into their minds. Five days later, absorbed in the game, his webbed hand moved hesitantly toward a piece on the board, a bishop, carved to look both haughty and bored.

"Yes" Atynleigh said, "that is the man I was going to move." She looked at him with astonishment. "Do you know where I wanted him to go?"

"A line." His claw hovered above the board in a diagonal. "Capturing a rook." The claw stopped above Mother's ward man, shaped like a Berserker, shown biting down on the top of his shield.

"Can you move it?"

Creature's golden eyes locked on Atynleigh's brown ones. She moved her head to encourage him. In response, his claws curled inward, moving them out of the way. He used the knuckles of the hand, just above the webbing, to grasp the bishop and deftly move it across the board, pushing the rook out of the way. He then carefully plucked up the rook and set it aside.

The room filled with Atynleigh's laughter. She and Mother both laughed—perhaps for the first time in months. This movement of a clawed hand from a healing stranger had made them feel a lightness that had been rare in their cabin.

It was at the end of his third week of recovery, during such a chess match, that the full danger of their situation closed around them. The match had barely started when Creature straightened his back, his eyes closed into slits, and focused on the door.

"They come."

Mother did not hesitate or question the creature. There was danger close and closing.

"Move. Make yourself as small as you can in the dark corner of Atynleigh's bed, back, under the slant of the roof."

"I can fight."

"You will lose. Do as I say."

When Mother used that tone, no one could withstand her. Atynleigh watched Creature roll back onto the small bed where it was wedged between the hang of the roof and the slant of the steps going to the loft where Mother slept.

Mother and daughter then pulled the rough blankets of Creature's pallet off the floor and threw them over the huddled figure of the lake-man, making a mess of unmade bed in the dark corner. They moved the low table with its chess board intact over the clean and flattened space where the pallet had been, roughing the dirt floor with their feet as well as they could. Mother scattered the wood fire enough to lower the light of the cabin just as they heard the men approach.

A fist pounded on the door.

"Who is there?" Mother called.

"The Reeve of the shire, Widow. Open."

Mother opened the door and let the firelight fill the entryway. There were three men dressed in rough tunics and wool capes. Two were men from the village. All were on foot. She glanced from the faces of the men she knew to the one she did not.

"Reeve Tomasil, it is late. Is there trouble?" She looked past them as if the trouble were waiting in the clearing.

"We come to warn of trouble. The fisherman here is certain there is sign of a Spirit Animal, wounded and ashore, in this area." Reeve Tomasil pushed the stranger forward as he spoke. It was as close to an introduction as was possible in this primitive community.

The stranger then spoke with a surly voice, trying to assert authority where he had none, "We need to inspect the houses. Make sure he isn't hiding."

Mother laughed and pushed the door wide open. "Look all you want, Reeve. But I think if I had seen a lake monster in my house, I would be seeking you instead of the other way around."

The stranger stepped forward and wrenched the door from Mother's hand.

"I'll have my own look around."

"No, sir. The Reeve may, but you shall not."

The stranger was shocked by this barrier to his wishes. He started to push past Mother but that proved to be a problem as the woman stood her ground.

"The Reeve is known to me and is welcome in this house. I do not allow that familiarity to every person. Certainly not a stranger who does not know a proper welcome." As Mother said this, she fixed the stranger with her eyes and seemed to grow both taller and straighter. For the first time all of them noticed that she had come to the door with a fish skinning knife in her strong right arm.

As the stranger took a short step back, Mother addressed the men she knew.

"Tomasil," Mother said trying to sound genuinely concerned, "has anyone been injured by this Spirit Animal? I could bring my medicines. You know I stand ready to help."

"No, Widow." The Reeve was weary of the long searches this stranger had insisted upon over the last weeks and he was not used to being offered help by the families he interrupted. It showed in his eyes and Mother now used that to seal a quick end to this visit. She spoke softly.

"You must be very tired. My daughter and I have a little left of our supper, but the rest is yours if you wish."

She stepped back from the doorway she had blocked to the stranger, and her act of generosity and openness had the effect she had counted on.

"No. No, we won't be staying, Widow. What little you have belongs to you and the child. We have warned you and checked the house. It is all we need."

"But it could be lurking..." the stranger tried to protest, but he was stopped by the tired Reeve.

"Our work is done here. We wish you a quiet evening, Widow."

"And a bright morning to you," Mother said.

Atynleigh joined her mother as they stood at the open door and watched the three men retreat down the path toward the village far out of sight. They stood in the lighted door just long enough to appear completely fearless and innocent, then closed the door, both shaking uncontrollably.

They stoked the fire to a bright blaze and slowly uncovered Creature. He too was shaking, but not from fear or cold.

It was a long time until his anger subsided. He spoke only with his mind that night.

"I must leave your house."

"You are not ready. We did not bring you this far to lose you out of fear—or anger."

"I put you in danger."

Mother hesitated, then stated a simple fact. "There is danger. True. And we do need to get you out of here. We were as lucky as we were smart tonight."

"Mother," said Atynleigh, her voice soft but earnest, "I have an answer, but it is a hard answer. We need to get Creature to the cliff hut. Even if the Reeve returned with men, Creature would see them and escape to the lake, down the cliff ropes long before anyone could walk the path."

Mother sat silently. The idea had occurred to her as well. The cliff hut was a small, barely functional shelter built on the top of the hill just to the west of their cabin. It had been built by Atynleigh's great-grandfather as part of a coastal warning system. An open fire on its heights could be seen far down the lake shore as well as inland. Such fires, passed from hilltop to hilltop, were a way to warn of marauders, though such times were now long past. The cliff ropes had been added years later so that careless people, caught on the small beach below during high tide, could climb to safety.

But how to get Creature to the hut? He had not been able to take more than a step or two across the dirt floor of the cabin. He fed himself, but only with food which had been presented to him. Yet, tonight's near miss had thrust the decision upon them all.

Somehow, Creature used the information in their minds to glean an accurate picture of the place and path.

"I can do this cliff path. But now, in the dark, before anyone sees us." Then he added with fierce resolve. "Or I must return to the lake, healed or not."

It was decided. It was done.

Slowly, with exhaustive effort, ever more frequent rests and moans of excruciating pain, the trio made their way from cabin to hut. Mother had gone ahead to lay a fire, prepare a pallet and bring up a sack of provisions, then returned to help Atynleigh guide and support Creature up, ever up.

"Child…" he had started once.

"Not now, Creature. We will talk when you are at the top."

But they had not talked then. Upon entering the hut Creature had collapsed half on and half off the pallet without word or sound of any kind.

Mother had insisted that both she and Atynleigh return to the cabin. After carefully tending the low fire and setting some dried fish within the reach of the lake man when—and if—he awoke, they returned to their home. They were in their beds just before daybreak, and still asleep at noon. During that entire time, a fog so thick it took one's breath away covered the entire cove, hiding both cabin and cliff.

That had been weeks ago, and now in the cold sunlight, Atynleigh ran toward the hut and the creature, who had become her friend.

Creature had risen clumsily from the rock upon which he had been sitting. The purplish scales of his face were gray at the tips and his jagged wound was a raw line that glowed white in the pale sun.

"I have rare medicine," Atynleigh said. "Mother trapped a beaver, and the musk glands have miraculous oils. She said you will feel the difference."

Atynleigh paused to look closely at the wound. It was raw, pink under pearl and as jagged as the thrust of the spear that he said had caused the near-fatal cut. Her hand moved close along its line but did not touch the fragile tissue. She sniffed at it.

"It doesn't smell. It is closing without infection."

"There is less pain. But the flesh is... stiff."

"That is how these things heal. We need to get you inside. Mother's salve will help."

Creature followed her into the hut and settled himself with a groan on a low stool.

"Let us see if this salve is the miracle Mother says it is."

She removed a pot of oily, amber-colored salve from her pack. It smelled strongly of musk and camphor. Her fingers took a dot of the thick gel from the pot and lightly moved it across the wound. Creature never moved, though she felt a long intake of breath through the gills on either side of his neck.

"Mother says you should feel a numbing tingle at first, but then relief. Do you understand?"

Creature nodded.

"She says it will speed the healing."

"That is good, child." He spoke these words in his whisper.

He always found Atynleigh's name to be too much a jumble of sound to attempt. She was just 'child' to him.

She put the pot of salve on the table. She had something she wanted to ask him.

"When my father was alive, he told me stories of the spirits that live in the great lake. He thought he saw you, or someone like you, once near the island at the west end of the lake. Father described a creature much like you."

"I seldom go to that island, but others like me find it comforting."

"Are there many of you?"

"Few. Fewer all the time."

"Are you the Spirit Animal that the tales talk of?"

"Spirit is too big a word. I am an animal, like you."

"I think you are the Spirit Animal of the fables." Atynleigh said this solemnly. She and Mother had talked about this. They were sure they knew who he was and much of what he was capable. "Do you bring the fish to our cove?"

"I can call them."

"We are grateful for that."

The creature did not smile, for his mouth was not capable of that, but Atynleigh felt a smile in what he said next, "Child, do you want to play the game? Or are we going to carve our own today?"

"Both. First we play."

In the days that had followed the difficult move to the cliff hut, while fall had inched toward early winter in the mountain community, Atynleigh and her Creature had started carving a new chess set, just for them.

The pieces were small, each one the length of one of Atynleigh's fingers. She fashioned the pieces as her father had, with curious little postures and attitudes. Her queen seemed worried and held her hand to her cheek. Atynleigh's king was vigilant, with a sword held across his knees. The bishops were looking for sin and sorrow with scowls on their faces.

Atynleigh had started not with any of these pieces, but with the knights. She knew they would be the hardest piece to capture, sitting on small, Nordic horses. They needed the extra width of the base of the precious walrus tusk, the last two her family had, so she began with her knights, and it was then that she made a stylistic decision that would affect every piece on the board.

She attacked the delicate ivory with purpose and precision. When she had finished the first knight, she held it out to Creature for inspection.

A bubbling sound much like a chortle came from Creature's throat.

He was looking at a chessman with the features of a man, riding a stout horse. But the eyes were remarkable. They were not the eyes of a man, but the round, bulging eyes of a fish, staring with a challenging intensity out of a human face. They were, unmistakably, the eyes of Creature, yet just human enough to make one assume that the carver either lacked skill or was making a joke.

Atynleigh and Creature's free time had passed in much this way—playing and carving. They were ready to start the last three pawns that stormy winter day. They would begin after they played their game of chess.

Perhaps it was the intervening slate of the hillside that interrupted Creature's sense of surrounding. Perhaps it was the soothing balm or strong camphor of the salve. Perhaps it was just his increasing contentment in Atynleigh's presence, or his intense efforts to expand the language between them, but Creature did not intuit the danger until it was too late.

The persistent stranger that had almost found them out in Mother's cabin had not forgotten his ill-treatment that night. When he received word of the abundance of fish on Mother's drying rack, he was certain that she knew more of the lake monster than she had shared. He had observed both the cabin and the hut from a distance. Smoke from the lofty cliff hut could not be explained save by the presence of an unknown. He had followed the daily trek of the child to the hut. And today he had chosen to make his secretive climb up the brushy, western side of the cliff. He would come upon them from the back side of the hill. If they ran down the eastern path, he could catch them easily—a young girl and lake man more used to water than land. The south side was an impenetrable tangle of brambles and berry bushes. North lay only the sheer drop to the lake, surely too great a fall with too shallow a bottom for even the creature to make that a viable choice. There would be no escape.

The stranger moved with cunning. As he raised his head above the slate rocks at the top of the cliff his presence became known in an instant but too late.

With a throaty hiss Creature rose with a speed that turned the inside of the hut into a shamble. The table, board and chessmen were overturned. Atynleigh's safety and escape became his only focus. Creature threw the door open and held it wide.

"Run, child."

Atynleigh understood a tone so forceful. She charged through the door and almost ran into the stranger as he appeared around the corner of the hut. He had a long knife in his hand and his instinct was to grab for the girl as she flew past him. His hand caught her sleeve and spun her to the ground.

That was his mistake.

"Monster," was the only word Atynleigh heard from the creature.

In the instant the stranger's attention had been turned to Atynleigh, Creature moved toward the assailant. He was slow but his bulk and returning strength were all he needed to grab the man's arm with one clawed hand, twisting it around his back and pushing him away from Atynleigh and toward the cliff.

At first the stranger tried to free himself, slashing backwards with the long knife. If any of the blows met flesh, they had no effect. Atynleigh was scrambling to her feet when she saw Creature straighten and twist hard on the man's arm. The bones of the stranger's arm cracked apart, followed by an anguished scream.

"Don't. Don't!" the man screamed, but Creature was pushing the evil presence steadily toward the cliff. At the edge of the precipice Creature lifted the stranger entirely off the ground.

With a mighty heave the stranger sailed off the cliff. A wailing cry followed his body down.

But there was still danger. Creature's efforts had brought him tottering too close to the edge. He reached out his right hand to steady himself on the single rocky protrusion near him. It should have been easy, but Atynleigh also saw the paroxysm of pain along the raw line of his wound. His arm reached out to steady himself on a rock, but the muscles contracted in pain, missing the rock. Gravity took Creature's body over the edge.

Atynleigh reached out to him in futile desperation. "No," she screamed.

She watched as Creature fell, haphazardly at first, then he straightened himself, arched his back, and rolled over. There was a shallow bottom to the cove here and he needed to enter at as horizontal a plane as possible while still cutting into the water. The impact was intense. She listened hard for one last thought, but if it was there, it trailed off before fully formed.

In the weeks that followed Atynleigh finished the chess set that she and Creature had made together. She and Mother played a single game with it, so that each piece knew its place and purpose. Then Atynleigh made a stone container of soft pumice and placed each piece carefully inside the hollow of it. She sealed the lid with wax and then made her way to the beach at the base of the cliff. On a thin strip of land well beyond the high tide line she buried the stone container deep in the soft sand.

"It is here," she said, "for us; a bridge across two lands."

For years, even after she grew to adulthood, with children and then grandchildren of her own, Atynleigh would come to this spot. She would sit near the chess set and talk to Creature, as though he were alive and lying in the shallows just off the cliff. Sometimes she was sure she could hear his soft words drift across the water to her. Always the same.

"Do good."

It is of note that for many years fish were a regular presence off the cabin by the great lake. It is also of note that the chess set was discovered hundreds of years after even Atynleigh's grandchildren had grown old and died. The Lewis Chessmen, as they are called, were found in 1831 on the shores of Lake Uig on the Isle of Lewis. They can now be seen in the British Royal Museum. They are beautifully carved, quite small, and have bulging, fish-like eyes.

See L.A.W. Butler's story "Her Spirit Animal"
online at Metaphorosis.
If you liked it, leave a comment. Authors love
that!
Remember to subscribe to our e-mail updates so
you'll know when new stories are posted.

About the story

Writers love to read. In June of 2019 I read an article in *Smithsonian Magazine* about the Lewis chessmen. This was a discovery of artfully carved chess pieces that were found buried in the sand on the Isle of Lewis. These pieces were carved sometime during the 12th century. My mind started to churn with an idea. Who carved the pieces? Why did they bury them so carefully in the sand? Throw in a little of the *Creature from the Black Lagoon* and *Beauty and the Beast* and a story is born.

A question for the author

Q: What do you think is the single most important quality for a good writer to possess?

A: Humility. There are a finite number of plot lines (usually numbered from five to seven) and everything you create is going to be a variation on those themes. It is how you play with those ideas, whom you choose to grapple with those conflicts, and the words you assign to each that make you a writer. That means you are sharing space with a great many talented people. Appreciate the fact that you are part of an amazing world of people who read, who write, and who value both.

About the author

Ms. Butler began writing speculative fiction in 7th grade after bingeing on a stack of Superman comics. Her academic background in both science and economics allows her to find many strange and wonderful places to put spunky girls and enlightened creatures of all kinds.

Tashala's Hair

Richard Strachan

For the novices of Kilavastin, the monastery's position high on the cold, north-facing flank of the mountain was enough to recommend it to even the most austere followers of the Path. The wind hared in over the plains from the ice fields in the distance, and most mornings would see the precincts dusted in a fine layering of silver frost. The chambers and cells and stone corridors were satisfyingly bleak, the windows shuttered only by thin partitions that rattled to the slightest breeze. The fire pits in the centre of each hall were lit to a strict and unyielding timetable: in the mornings, so the novices could brew their tea; and in the evenings, so their robes could be washed in great copper cauldrons and laid out overnight to dry. Meals were plain fare and luxuries were permitted only on the most sacred days. At the Feast of the Climbing Reed, the novices were granted a whole cup of fermented milk, and the evening of Crane Fall saw them lavishly stuff themselves with the first of the preserved fruit from the previous autumn.

It was a life of rigour and hardship, but few complained. In many ways it was an improvement over the quality of the lives they had known before, in families that scratched a dusty living from the dry fields of the south, where the waters of the valleys were acrid and slow. Out there, raids from the *anernath*, those horned and bloodthirsty daemons, were becoming more and more frequent. Kilavastin was a refuge from such hardship, and more than a refuge. High on the flank of the Tongue of Fire, the monastery was like a mouth shouting its prayers into the firmament, hollering to the twin moons of Aixe and Kast as they gazed down in pious approval. And when was a better time for the balm of prayer than when the land lay in such desperate straits, plagued by drought and poverty and war?

This was certainly what Gan thought, knuckling the sleep from his eye as he made his way to the meditation terrace on the edge of the monastery. His mother and father were reed weavers and they lived in a one-room shack on the lip of a dried-out lake, ten miles from the rocky foothills of the mountain. A day with a full stomach was one to mark on the village stele. When they had seen that he could decipher the prayers and blessings written by the mendicant priests whenever they passed through, his parents decided to send him to the monastery. High piety and low common sense found their complement in each other; one fewer of their many mouths to feed could only be a good thing, and for that mouth to be raised in prayer would double the benefit.

Gan had not seen them in five years. He didn't know whether they still wove their living from the dying reeds or whether they had passed away into the firmament above, but he gave thanks to them all the same. Kilavastin was shelter and a guaranteed meal, and freedom from the threat of bandit raids or the dark attention of the horned ones to the west.

More than that, it was a whetstone to a sharpening mind. He had always known he was a cut above the folk in his village and his life here was just the tangible proof. He would take all he wanted from Kilavastin. In time he would sit where the abbot sat each day to give them their lessons. He had no doubt, none at all. The scriptures of the Path might say that *Doubt is the lathe of certainty*, but Gan had no need of it. If the other novices were no more than cluttered collections of gathered wood, then he was already the carven chair. And as the scriptures also said, *Let each thing that is made be made for its own purpose*, and for what other purpose could Gan have been made but this?

He was a thin, reedy boy, his black hair shaven to the scalp. He was tall, although he made himself seem smaller by his hunkered, creeping gait as he passed through the corridors. His rope-soled sandals made no noise on the stone floor and the doors of the other cells, stained black with time, were still closed. Gan always made sure to be first up. It was a skill to wake before the rising sun. If you wanted to distinguish yourself, he had always thought, then it paid for your enthusiasm to be seen.

The steel morning was still glazed with the indigo of night as the sun began to rise. There was a smell in the air of frost and unleavened bread, the scent of rosemary, the acrid tang of brewed tea and mountain flowers. The terrace was empty when he reached it, the low dais at the southern end untenanted. Gan settled himself near the dais, sitting cross-legged on the stone and gnawing furtively on a crust of bread he had hidden in his robes. It would not be long before the other novices arrived to hear the abbot speak. Bread finished, the hard lump of it yielding to his throat, he closed his eyes and adopted a posture of meditation. He smoothed his brow, drew his mouth down slightly as if to indicate some knotty issue that he hadn't quite resolved.

His eyes looked onto the darkness inside him. He thought unbidden of his mother's face, his father's bare and field-stained feet standing on the rushes of their hut.

He heard Quath and Hart come scuffling from the corridor into the open air, stifling deep, lung-laden yawns. The rustle of their white cotton robes, the scrape of their sandals against the flagstones. He could imagine the smoky plume of their breath in the cold morning air.

"*The weasel hunts when the sun is young,*" Hart quoted in a whisper designed to carry. Quath giggled. Gan could hear him scratching at the lice in his hair. They were all due another shave soon. Gan inclined his head, acknowledging, but he didn't open his eyes.

"*The poppy drinks the morning's perfume,*" he answered in a still, clear voice, "*while the cactus slumbers.*"

Hart snorted through his nose and padded down behind him. Gan felt Hart's rough finger prod into his back.

"Cactus. That's the best you've got, eh?" he sneered.

"Well, the spines of the cactus are sharp and must be avoided," Gan said without turning his head. "And you certainly are a prick ..."

Quath bellowed with laughter. Gan opened his eyes and allowed himself a smile, although he knew he would pay for it later. He could feel Hart's rich displeasure behind him. He was a lumpy, ill-featured boy, not one to let an insult go unpaid.

"*You're* the prick!" Hart hissed. The finger came prodding in again to Gan's back. "The daemons take you, and your mother," he said.

"Your mother *is* a daemon," Gan retorted. "And your father pleasures himself on her horn every night."

"Stop, Gan!" Quath choked. "You dole out insults like a rich man dispensing alms! My bowl is full!"

Hart's voice came low and serious into Gan's left ear. He could smell the boy's breath, still rich with sleep. "You're a wilful one, aren't you? At least I don't pleasure the Egg in his cell every afternoon ... How do you like the feel of *his* horn, eh?"

The insult quivered in the air like a struck chord. Gan felt a wash of heat sweep over him. He remembered the precept, *Emotions are the tether of the clay*, and said nothing. He was taller than Hart and had the greater reach, although Hart had weight and solidity on his side. They had never fought, but even so, he wasn't entirely sure that Hart would win. Despite the discipline of the switch and the leather strap, scuffles were common enough amongst the boys. Even so, he would not turn and strike.

Hart, emboldened, laughed with false mirth. If he had any further insult in his mouth though, he kept it to himself as the other novices began to file into the terrace, slumped in their white robes and still heavy with sleep. The initiates, younger boys with bare feet dressed in sky-blue tunics, filed in to sit on the very cusp of the terrace where it fell away into the open air.

A hush fell over the novices as the Egg hobbled in from the western cloister. The ripple of their talk faded away, until the only sound across the precinct was the high whisper of the northern breeze and the quiet tread of the abbot's sandals as he climbed with effort onto the dais.

All bowed their heads, although Gan glanced up under his brows to watch the Egg limp slowly to the reed mat. The dome of his head was smooth and hairless; even the eyebrows and the eyelashes seemed to have faded with age, as sparse as winter grass. There was not a hair on his chin or lip, and his blue-veined legs, dark with bruises, were as thin as rope. He gathered his green robes about him and settled into position, coughing tremulously, his eyes milky white. His age-gnarled hands were cupped in his lap. Gan felt the white eyes draw across him as the abbot gazed out at the gathered crowd, all of them sitting patiently on the terrace waiting for him to begin.

The Egg saw everything, it was said. The fog of age might have laid its cloud across his vision, but that did not mean his sight was not clear. Gan certainly hoped so. He hoped the Egg could see the need in him. Every afternoon, he knelt at the door to the abbot's cell, waiting to make himself conspicuously useful. Small errands, help with letters, filling the Egg's water cup, brewing his tea — anything in exchange for whatever crumb of insight the abbot might let drop from his table. Knowledge was as food and drink to Gan, and he would take his fill. More than that, it was the coin of progress, and he would earn his keep. He wanted to make the abbot proud, to show him everything he had learned at his feet.

One day, he thought. *One day, I will sit where you sit now.*

As was the purpose of the lesson, the abbot waited until the novices felt emboldened enough to ask for a particular story. Tales from scripture or cosmology or from the Golden Precepts; tales of myth and legend and history; tales that would illuminate the soul's endlessly refined condition in the ocean of eternity. Tales were the weft and weave of Kilavastin. They were how the monks and the initiates made sense of the world. Kilavastin itself, the monastery that sat atop the Tongue of Fire, was the tale that was told about it as much as anything else. Everybody knew of Kilavastin, where the first steps of the Path had once been taken. Here was where the words of the Way had first been spoken, and what was the Way but a story about how to live?

The cold air slithered over Gan's bare shoulder. He prepared himself to speak — as everyone knew he would. It had almost become a tradition that no one would break the abbot's silence until Gan had sallied forth with his first question. But then, breaking the hush, his voice braying in the morning air, Hart stepped suddenly into the gap instead.

"Please, master," he said. "This unworthy one has a request he would humbly make?"

The Egg made no outward show of having heard. He sat there, all folded up into himself like a woven basket. Then, after a moment, the gesture visible only as a faint tremble in his jaw, the Egg nodded. Hart went on.

"I have heard — *we* have heard — that the *anernath* make great gains against the people, and that the lands groan under the weight of their evil. I thought there might be a tale that would speak to us in this time? In the scriptures it says, *Those who would counter evil must first make themselves pure*, and I thought perhaps the tale of the Peerless Knights might give us courage and inspiration? For who could be purer than the Peerless Knights, or we novices of the monastery who dedicate ourselves to the Path?"

There was a ripple of suppressed laughter. Even the most pious initiate would have trouble describing his fellows as being exactly *pure* …

Gan masked his smile in case the Egg should happen to see. He flitted through the verses in his mind until he came to the passage Hart's words had conjured up.

"Please, master," he said sharply, arm raised. "This unworthy one also has a tale in mind, for which he would humbly ask so we can be illuminated by its wisdom."

The white gaze of the Egg slid swiftly across Gan's face. Gan bowed his head.

He could hear Hart breathing heavily through his nose behind him.

The Egg's voice was perhaps the most remarkable thing about him, and when he spoke, Gan felt the words thrum and settle across the still, empty air. For all his frailty, it was a voice of resonance and power, like a velvet note blown through the body of an oboe. He seemed able to project it to any part of the precinct with the same subtle force.

"Would you have your tale, novice," he said, "before your fellow's? Remember, it is said that *All things must be answered in their proper order.*"

More laughter, but Gan had expected this. He countered swiftly with:

"But is it not also said, master, that *The seed must be blown by a contrary wind to settle?*"

Across the precinct he could hear the indrawn breath from the other novices, the respectful laugh at his audacity. On the Egg's face there was the faintest twitch of a reaction, a flicker of the lip.

"If you seek only to illuminate your fellow's request with your own," he said, "be bold enough to ask it."

"I believe the story I have in mind would better reflect the inspiration my fellow seeks. The Peerless Knights are, after all, *peerless*, and we could never assume to attain their level of purity. I seek only our enlightenment in requesting this, though I confess the tale is one that I would much like to hear. It has always moved me."

He bowed deeper. He could practically hear Hart's teeth grinding in his jaw behind him. Quath tittered uneasily, whispered: "Oh, he'll get you for this, Gan! He'll *get* you!"

But Gan paid no mind. He had reward enough, as he glanced up, in seeing the faint curve of the abbot's lip, the glint of a revealed tooth.

"And what tale did you have in mind, novice?"

"Please, master," Gan said. "This unworthy one would beseech you to enlighten us with the tale of King Raden. I believe it would shed light on the low desire for great things that my fellow's request, perhaps unwittingly, has revealed."

The Egg paused. The hands shifted in his lap. "And what do you know of this tale, novice?"

Gan swallowed. It was a tale his mother had told him when he was young, before he went to sleep; when the dusk stroked the fields with purple fire, and when the moons of Aixe and Kast began their graceful dance through the vault of night. But he would never admit as such here, of course. He would never hear the end of it from the other novices.

"Please, master," he said. "I know only as much as my nature has permitted me to know, for my head teems with half-remembered tales. After all, is it not said that *The clay vessel cannot be overfilled*?"

The abbot, to much general astonishment, gave a short, flat bark of a laugh. Never had the Egg laughed in their presence before. Gan felt a strange tenderness then, that he had so moved him. The other novices almost imperceptibly leaned forward; if Gan had managed to so sting the Egg, then it stood to reason that the abbot's words would be worth listening to.

"Very well," he said to the gathered crowd. Hunched on the dais like that, he looked more like a little woven basket than ever. 'Let us have the tale of King Raden then, and see if his travails cannot illuminate the 'low desire for great things' which the novice here has identified ..."

In those days (the abbot said), far to the north, there was a great kingdom known as the Kingdom of Sabaenea, and King Raden ruled there in justice and temperance. The eastern lines of that kingdom stretched all the way to the sea, and the southern fringes covered what are now the borders of our own lands. Indeed, Kilavastin itself was part of its domain in those days.

Raden was a just king, beloved of his people, but it was his curse to be born in dark times. The *anernath* were already breaking from the earth of the western lands, spewing up from the pits of fire that wise men tell us boil at the very centre of the earth. Villages and towns fell to the flame of their swords, Men, women, and children were used most horribly in their dread rituals. Pirates raided far to the east, and for three years in a row the crops failed before the harvest. Drought and famine and war — the three signs of a changing time were upon him, and even the most just king has to bow before the signs he is given. Age was growing more heavily on King Raden, day after day, and

he knew that his reign would soon come
to an end. It could either end in the fire
and slaughter of war against the
daemons, or it could continue in fear and
safety as long as the *anernath* suffered
them to live. All he knew was that he
could not be the king to lead his country
onwards into whatever fate awaited it.

King Raden had a son, Janna, the
prince who in the normal course of things
would inherit Sabaenea on Raden's death.
It was in King Raden's mind to abdicate
his responsibilities and pass them on to a
younger man, one better suited to the
rigours to the age, but the thought made
him most uneasy. He loved his son, but
King Raden was wise and saw far, and he
knew that Janna was the kind of man
who might treat a kingdom as no more
than the spoils of his own vanity. Janna
was young and confident and strong, most
fair to look upon, but those who have
never had to struggle often lack the
resilience to make hard decisions. There
was ambition in him too. Ambition can
often be yoked to a finer purpose, but
there was a streak of cruelty in Janna
that King Raden had long tried to ignore.
The prince, it was said, took rather too
much enjoyment in beating his hunting

dogs, and he treated his servants little better.

One morning, King Raden's daughter, Princess Tashala, came to him. A silk veil covered eyes that had been sorely weeping, but the king was at first so preoccupied with his own concerns that he did not notice her distress. Then, when she drew back the veil and he saw the sorrow on her face, he bade her sit and called for wine.

"What ails you, daughter?" he asked.

Princess Tashala sipped her wine and dried her eyes. She was a striking figure, fine-boned, tall, her long black hair breaking the bounds of the silken cords she had used to tie it up.

"Oh father!" she cried. "You must flee from here, while you still have the chance. Fear grips me in its chains, and I know for a very fact that your life is in danger."

"Our lives are only given us for our allotted span," King Raden said. "But tell me daughter, what makes you think I am at risk in the very centre of my kingdom? War draws near, I have no doubt, but it is not yet upon us."

And then Princess Tashala told her father all that she had heard from the lips of her own brother. Prince Janna, who had no greater store of patience than he had of compassion, could not wait for his father to die in the natural course of things. He wanted the crown of Sabaenea now, for his very own, and he had boasted of such to Tashala — for, despite the differences between them, brother and sister were very close, and had been since they were children. No more than ten months separated their births, although Tashala's arrival had killed the mother Janna spent the rest of his life mourning. Often, King Raden wondered if the sad death of his wife was what had made his children's relationship both so feverishly close, and so unusually overwrought.

"You must believe that this is no idle threat. Janna means to kill you and seize the crown, and then by the light of the Path that guides us I cannot say what mayhem he will inflict upon the kingdom. He has long waited for this moment, father, and those whose hearts are so torn by desire will never make kind kings. Forgive me for bringing you such distress, but I fear that he would even take me for a bride, so twisted by his lust for power has he become. He has always blamed me for mother's death, has he not, and now at last he will find a way to punish me for it!"

Now, King Raden, although struck deeply by these terrible words, was above all things wise. He knew that his daughter spoke the truth, for although she was in many ways a wilful and haughty character, she had a streak of iron in her that would not bend or break. If she had been made so distraught by what she had heard, then he knew that a moment of great seriousness was upon him.

Ask yourself what a king should do in such a trial. No one would have blamed him for dragging his son to his dungeons and ending the threat to his kingdom on the edge of the executioner's blade. But although King Raden was wise and just, he was also a father. He could not kill his own son. Still less could he allow his son to become a murderer and kill his own father. Despite it all, he loved Prince Janna. The boy was his own flesh and blood, and who can think of their own flesh and blood as irredeemable?

Some, of course, would say that this was a terrible weakness, and that kings must put aside such mortal concerns if they are to rule with strength; for all things, even the love of a father for his

son, must be subordinate to the needs of
the kingdom. But the king, who knew his
scriptures, also knew that weakness could
be turned into strength, for is it not said
that, *The green shoot can be plucked with
ease from the soil, and yet given time can
crack the very mountains*? In the same
way a newborn child placed into its
father's arms soothes the beast inside
him, perhaps a kingdom placed in Janna's
hands would cool the fire of his strange
hatreds. The kingdom would be saved and
Tashala would no longer suffer her
brother's unnatural attention — or at
least, so Raden hoped.

He summoned Janna that evening.
Having taken himself from the gambling
table or from the arms of his courtesans,
the prince strode into the throne room
with all the arrogance of youth. He saw
his father sitting there on the throne of
Sabaenea, his head encircled by
Sabaenea's crown, and all he saw was an
old man too weak to look his son in the
eye.

Now, as I have said, Sabaenea was a
rich and powerful kingdom, and the
throne room reflected all its strength and
majesty. The throne itself was of solid
gold, with a cresting rail of jewel-

encrusted silver. Rubies and emeralds sparkled from the arms, and the dais on which it sat was mantled in purple velvet. The long apron of the dais was guarded by the warriors of the king's personal guard, giants near seven feet tall bearing ivory-hilted glaives, their heads capped with steel helmets. The room itself was larger than any lord's banqueting hall, hundreds of feet from end to end. The walls held bas-reliefs of sculpted marble, depicting the legends of Sabaenea's long and storied history, and the ceiling was a wondrous display of frescoes that celebrated the great victories of its armies. Raden was not a proud man, but he wanted his son to be certain that Raden was speaking to him not just as a father, but as a king, and that the decision he was about to make was coming from a position of the most unassailable power.

"You wished to see me, father?" Prince Janna drawled.

He wore his armour, the king noted; a gilded breastplate, a sword at his hip. The young man stood there as if he had spent half his day perfecting the pose, but King Raden saw far into his son's hidden heart. The boy was anxious too. He had achieved nothing in his own short life and in a way he felt the shame of his privilege. He had never been given the chance to prove himself. All this splendour had hung in front of him all the days of his life, and who can live with such temptation and not become deformed by it?

"Indeed, my son," the king said. He leaned forward in the throne, felt the weight of that golden circlet on his head, as he had felt it every day of his reign. "I summoned you here to give you something which I know you have long desired, which turns and twists in your mind day and night, and which I am convinced in the end you will not thank me for giving you."

Prince Janna glanced at his father's face, so grave and heavy with unspoken sorrows. "I thank you, father," he said carefully, "although I confess this does not sound like the sort of gift a man may happily receive."

"It is not," the king said, bluntly. "And yet, I would give it to you all the same. I would save you from a course of action that would draw you far from the Path that guides us all, and then Sabaenea and your beloved sister must suffer the consequences of a father's love, for good or ill."

"You will have my gratitude regardless," Prince Janna said. He bowed with a restrained flourish. "You know how much I value any gift from you, father …"

King Raden summoned his advisors and ministers, the heads of his armies, his chancellors and priests. He bade all of them witness, and then he removed the crown from his head and passed it to Prince Janna — King Janna, as he now was.

It is said that a monarch must take the crown with reluctance, in recognition of the hard duty thrust upon them, but Janna could not help himself. He snatched the circlet from his father's hands like a child grabbing a sweetmeat from his nurse, so eagerly had he waited for this moment. After placing the crown on his head, Janna practically dragged his father from the throne.

With heavy steps, Raden plodded down the dais to the floor, pushing past the giants of his personal guard — now King Janna's personal guard, sworn to protect the king's life with their own.

"Is it done?" Janna asked, his eyes blazing. A smile flickered across his thin and handsome face. He looked, Raden thought, like the boy he had once been, eager for the games to begin on his birthday. "Is it right, am I now king?"

He looked pleadingly to the priests, the advisors, the generals, as if scared that they would contradict him. All of them, with the briefest of glances at the worn figure of Raden, who seemed to have diminished in only the few minutes since his son had entered the throne room, nodded their assent. It was done.

"All hail the king," they cried as one.

"How mother would be pleased to see me now ..." Janna whispered. Then he turned to the court and proclaimed: "There will be a change now in this kingdom, I swear it!" He grasped the sceptre, clutched at the hilt of his sword. "No more shall we skulk behind our walls in fear of battle. No more shall we let the daemons of the west press against our borders, killing the kinfolk of our neighbours. No longer shall the people go hungry from famine and drought. Open the granaries," he commanded. "Raise my armies! Let every strong man and woman of Sabaenea take up the sword and prepare for war. Sabaenea will meet the challenges that face it head on, and we shall be victorious!"

Raden lowered his eyes. How to tell his son that the granaries were empty, that there were not weapons enough to arm his soldiers? How to tell him that the duties of kingship were to balance so many competing demands that a successful king was more like a pilot weaving a ship through the reefs and sandbars of a treacherous harbour, rather than one who sets a single course and takes it? He would find out for himself, in time …

"And one final command I make today," King Janna declared. He raised the sceptre and pointed it at his father. There was the briefest moment in his eyes, the quickest flash of horror at the step he was about to take, but it was soon gone. "Guards — arrest this man. His failures have led us to the brink of ruin, and he will not go unpunished."

And so the guards, who not five minutes before would have given their lives for him, took Raden in hand and cast him down into the dungeons of the king's palace, there to await the king's pleasure. It was no less than he had expected.

The dungeons were not as fearful or as grim as that word would lead you to expect. A dungeon is merely a place to keep a prisoner until they can be dealt

with, and the simple loss of liberty is
torment enough. The cell in which Raden
was thrown was simple and bare, but not
needlessly grotesque. It contained no
more than a plain wooden bed and a hole
in the ground for a toilet, but the floor was
well-swept   and   the   walls   cleanly
whitewashed. A barred window high on
the eastern wall admitted the sunlight at
dawn, and there was a thick woollen
blanket for Raden to keep himself warm.
He did not know what Janna planned to
do with him, but reasoned that there was
no   point   in   tormenting   himself   with
conjecture. All would become clear in
time. Settling himself on the bed, Raden
began to think back to his lessons in
scripture, sending his mind to wander
along the clear and uncluttered avenues
of the Path, where none could touch it,
while his body waited uneasily for the
king's judgement. He thought of Tashala,
his daughter, and hoped against hope
that he had not made a terrible mistake.

The first day passed in silence. The
sunlight   swung   leisurely   across   the
whitewashed wall, painting the bricks in
gold and amber. Raden heard nothing
from the other cells and saw no sign of his
gaoler. No one brought him food or drink,

or unhooked the slat in the cell door to check if he was well. *No matter,* Raden thought. *Many are the people in Sabaenea who lack food in these dark times, and I should not complain if for once my stomach feels the pangs of an unaccustomed hunger.*

But the next day passed in the same way, and still no one came to his cell. A man can be humbled through lack of food for a few days at least, but he cannot be humbled long through lack of water. Despite himself, Raden stood by the slat in the door and called for sustenance, but no one answered. He had been dragged to the dungeons, it seemed, to be forgotten.

Days and nights passed. Raden could imagine King Janna frantic with indecision over what he should do, finally paralysed into this cruel indifference. Janna hated his father for standing so long in his way. He loved his father for standing aside and giving him the crown. He hated his sister for killing their mother. He loved his sister because in some way she was all of his mother he had left. What awful conflictions had gone into this boy, Raden sighed, and how blind had he been to think that charity would smooth out these flaws.

He licked the moisture from the walls where it gathered on the brick. He cursed the clemency that had made these dungeons less foul than they could have been, for there were no rats he could trap for food. His stomach writhed with agony and his throat burned with thirst, and slowly he felt what little strength remained to him start to fade. And yet even now, after everything, he did not regret the decision he had made. His son might be killing him by inches, but he was not yet a murderer.

He could not say how much time passed before he received his first visitor. Each day dragged from dawn to dusk, changeless and austere. In the end, it was not Janna who came to see him, or any functionary of the dungeons, but Princess Tashala, who had spent every day since Janna's succession begging the new king to allow her to see her father. Whether through guilt about what he had done, or simple love for his sister, Janna had finally agreed.

She appeared in that drear place like a glimpse of sunlight in a cloudy sky, her silks as vibrant as the flowers in the fields, her jewels glittering like stars. More dazzling than either was the love Raden saw in her eyes, the sorrow and the pity as she took his weakened body in her arms and sat with him on the bed.

"My lord, you cannot understand the grief a daughter feels when she sees her father brought so low," she said. "My heart is heavier than stone. Janna is surely cursed if he treats you so abominably."

"Forgive your brother," Raden managed to say. His voice was as dry as the autumn leaves that clattered about the forecourts of the palace. "After all, he has not killed me yet. Janna has never had to make a decision in his life before, and he only does what he does now for the good of the kingdom, I am sure. A crown must forget those who wore it before, as it cleaves to him who wears it now."

"He does what he does only for his own good, of *that* I have no doubt," Tashala scorned. "Even now he talks more of our marriage than he does of the duties of a king. He claims his love for me is pure, but it is only the love of a greedy man for that which he cannot have. And I swear, on our wedding night I will claw the eyes from his head rather than let him use me in such a disgusting violation of the Way!"

It grieved Raden deeply to hear this. Truly, he began to realise the scale of his error. He had given Janna the crown to prevent his son being consumed by his desires, but was his own need to protect his son not just another kind of desire in its way? The scriptures were surely true when they said that desire was the snare at the side of the road to peace. The laws of Sabaenea, laid down an age ago when the world was young, could not countenance the crown being passed to any but the first born. Raden saw those laws now as great tendrils snaking out from the shadows of history and binding his hands to a decision he wished he had not made. But what can a father do against the love he bears his children?

Raden felt his spirits lower even further when he realised that his daughter carried no sustenance for him.

"Indeed not, father," she said. "Janna's guards searched me before I entered, and I was expressly forbidden from bringing you food or drink. I think he means for you to starve to death in here because he does not have the courage to wield the blade himself."

"Then leave me now," Raden said, "and let an old man suffer the punishment of his folly."

It was then that Tashala unwrapped the scarves that kept her long black hair tied up from her shoulders. She shook it free and Raden saw that it glistened with oils. He could smell a light fragrance of honey and cinnamon wafting through the cell. Tashala took up a lock of that hair in both her hands and held it out to him.

"But I knew how vindictive my brother could be," she said, offering it to him in all reverence. "Please. Sustain yourself."

Suddenly he understood what she had done. As Tashala cradled him to her breast, holding him as he would have held her when she was a child, Raden took his daughter's hair into his mouth and sucked and sucked, drawing the lacquered syrups from it. Lock by lock, he drank the sustenance she had prepared for him, the nourishment she had disguised in the oiled tresses of her hair. Slowly he felt a flicker of his old strength returning. The darkness that had been growing around the edges of his sight receded. The cold which he had felt creeping ever nearer in his lonely cell began to slacken.

"Feed from me," Tashala whispered into the silence, and the only sound was the soft papping of Raden's lips as he sucked the oils dry. "Feed, and be whole once more."

She had saved his life, of that there could be no doubt. Glazing her hair with nutrients, her locks plump with rich greases, Tashala came to his cell whenever she could, and whenever Janna's malicious caprice turned for a moment to a kind of mercy. Sometimes a day or two would pass, sometimes longer. When at last he heard the grinding click of the lock on his cell door, Tashala would rustle in with a sweep of her gilded silks and unravel the scarves from her head. Raden would fall into his daughter's arms as she uncoiled the great loops and oiled plaits of her raven-black hair, and he would gather them up and swoon at the heady scents of cinnamon and burnt sugar. It was all he could do not to choke himself on each strand as he eagerly sucked it into his mouth, drawing as much of the goodness from it as he could.

The risks Tashala was taking were a marvel to him, her bravery an example he tried to honour. Truly she walked the Path in righteousness, and not for the first time

Raden wished that this brave and resourceful young woman had been his first-born child instead of the callow young man he was now ashamed to call his son. The Law was all, Raden had thought in his foolishness. But are men and women made to serve the Law, or is the Law made to serve men and women instead?

As he sat in his bare cell, day after day, meditating on the Path and on all the varied steps that had led him to this moment, Raden tried not to imagine his son's confusion that his father yet lived. If his mother had lived, perhaps … Would there still be such an absence in his boy, such bewilderment and vice?

And then, months after Raden had abdicated, King Janna came at last to the dungeons of his palace to visit his father.

He bade his guards wait outside, those seven-foot giants who had once guarded Raden himself. His breastplate was glazed with dust, notched here and there by sword cut or axe blade, and his lean and once-handsome face was drawn with strain. His hand flexed on the hilt of his sheathed sword. Raden sat on the edge of his cot and watched his son, and for a moment it seemed as if their places had been reversed; that Janna, worn out with guilt and strife, had been thrown into the dungeon while Raden sat patiently to await his excuses.

"I confess it surprises me to find you still alive, father," the young king said. His voice cracked as he spoke, brittle with fatigue. "I have Tashala to thank for that, I suspect. I don't know how she has done it, but she is ever wilful."

"She honours me with her loyalty," Raden said, without malice. "And she honours the Path. Perhaps she hopes I can still intercede with you, and turn aside your foul desire to marry her."

Janna flinched. He rubbed the dust from his eye and seemed to reel for a moment. Again came to Raden that image of him as a boy, crying at some childish injustice.

"I see the hatred in her, every time I look on her face," he mumbled. "I thought us closer than any two people in the world, but I suspect I have deluded myself on this, as I have on so much else. I am not so arrogant or selfish as you have long assumed me, father."

"Then you no longer torment her with your attentions?"

"Let us say that I have postponed our marriage until the war is won. I will persuade her with my victory, and ..." He strode from one side of the cell to the other. He was unable to meet his father's eye, and when he spoke it was as if he were speaking to himself. "A victory which I confess seems further away than I would have ever thought possible ..."

"You seem surprised to find war a complex and unpredictable thing," Raden told him. "Reasons why I always strove to avoid it. Nothing overwhelms like war."

Janna gave a flat and mirthless laugh. He wiped his eye again and Raden realised that he was brushing away tears.

"Complex and unpredictable, and expensive beyond all measure ..."

"Why do you come here, my son?" Raden asked him gently. "Do you seek to torment me further, or is that blade on your hip designed to end my suffering at last?"

Janna rounded on his father, but there was no rage or anger in his expression. There was only the dark despair of someone pushed beyond his limits, and suddenly aware of what those limits actually were. When he spoke, it was as if he dreaded anyone overhearing what he had to say.

"In the name of the Path we follow," he sobbed, "what do I do? I thought the *anernath* merely some kind of savage beast, but they are things of smoke and midnight, utterly without mercy ... There is rebellion in the north, and there are thousands — *thousands* — of people dead from the plague in the east. The granaries are almost empty, we cannot raise money fast enough to pay the army, and our defeats multiply like locusts in the hot season. It is all streaming through my fingers, father, and I cannot keep hold of it! Please, what do I *do?*"

Raden looked at his son, not without pity. To have striven for so long, to have locked all his hopes into the box of one desire, and then to find that desire no more than a scattering of ashes that drifted through the air, elusive ... Janna had found the limits of his own capabilities, and they had shocked him.

"Is the crown something you still want?" Raden looked his son in the eye, and that lean face twisted as if struck. "Would you clutch power to you still, or would you freely give it up?"

The choice, if it was a choice, wrestled across Janna's face. He clawed at his breastplate as if trying to stop the power flying away from him. Desire and surrender were weighed in the balance of his heart; but in the end, one must always be heavier than the other.

"I would keep it still," he whispered. His face was pale, as if he couldn't believe the decision he had just made. "More than my mother alive, or Tashala at my side, it is the only thing I have ever truly wanted."

"Then I cannot help you," Raden said sadly. "And the only advice I can give is that what holds you in fetters must be given away. The only gift worth giving is that which is truly valued, and that which is still desired by the giver is no gift at all."

"This is the advice you give me," Janna wept. "My own father, who would see Sabaenea in ruins rather than lift his hand to help!"

"You have my help," Raden told him. "You must unshackle your desire for power, and give it away to one more worthy. Only then will you be saved, and Sabaenea with you."

With a cry of rage, Janna drew the first blue inch of steel from his scabbard. Raden sat there impassive, waiting for the blow to fall, but Janna did not swing the blade. He sobbed once, reeled back as the tides of his anger broke against the shore of his father's indifference — for truly, Raden had made his peace with life and had reached the end of his Path. After all, Life must be capped with Death, and the wise man makes sure to meet Death's eye when it approaches. For Janna though, Death was not yet a figure he could compass. He was young enough to think that Death could always be outfought.

"Go," Janna said in a hoarse voice. He swung the cell door open and stumbled out into the corridor. "Leave this place. Find whatever refuge you can, before it is all pulled down in ruins about our heads."

"May your Path be free of pain and hurdle, my son." Raden said. In the doorway he paused to rest his hand on his son's trembling shoulder. "I will go south to Kilavastin. You will find me there, when the time comes."

"Forgive me, father," Janna choked. "But if I ever see you again, I will kill you for all that you have done to me."

And thus parted father and son, King Raden and Prince Janna, or King Janna as he was still for a little while after that. And as Raden left his cell and then the palace grounds, he knew more than ever that to hold something close which you cannot easily give up is to be held in chains, locked in a dungeon deeper and more impenetrable than the one he had just left. When desire is your master, then the Path is made ever more obscure.

The dawn had long since burned away by the time the Egg finished. The cold breeze had tempered a degree or two, and the novices' bellies rumbled as the time of the day meal grew close. There was a sharp smell in the air of herbs and spices from the pottage bubbling in the cookpots. Soon the rigours of the day would properly begin.

"That is it," the Egg declared. "The story of King Raden, and how he was nourished on Tashala's hair, and how a kingdom was given away because of desire. Greed is ever a danger on the Path," he said. "Go now, and think on this."

His white eyes swept over the gathered novices as the story sank into them, and for the briefest moment they rested on

Gan, as if to say: *Heed these words, haughty one; for they are for you alone.*

Gan joined the others as they filed from the terrace, looking back to see the Egg still sitting there on the dais, his papery bald head bowed, his blue-veined legs still crossed. Gan wanted to go to him, to ask more, to learn more, to be of service. *All I want is to learn,* Gan wanted to tell him. *What else could be told of King Raden and Prince Janna? Did Raden ever make it to Kilavastin? What happened to Princess Tashala once her father left? Did King Janna die in battle, in his war against the daemons? Did he regret the clemency he had shown to his father at the end?* When his mother had told him the story, it had always ended with King Raden forgiving his son and leaving his cell to become a saint of the Way, performing miracles in the ruins of Sabaenea. Was this King Raden's fate? It made him feel uneasy not to know.

But once a question had been answered, it was not permitted to be reframed and it was up to the novices to parse the meaning from it. The Egg had spoken. That was all there was to it.

Precepts and orders and rules did not stop Gan's mind from pivoting uneasily around the story for the rest of the day, though. There were lessons in it for him, he knew. He just had to find them. Sabaenea had fallen many years ago and the war with the daemons was something that had lasted as long as people could remember. Some said that it would never end, because how could things of smoke and midnight ever be defeated by human arts? Perhaps in the end, he thought, Kilavastin itself would fall to them.

But no, it was impossible to imagine such a thing. As Gan washed the empty bowls when the day meal was done, his hands plunged into the tepid water of the kitchen sinks, he couldn't imagine the monastery falling into the same ruin as Sabaenea. It was eternal, surely. It was the cap of the mountain, the crown of the Path. It was the place that was woven of stories, and it would never fall as long as there were monks to learn them.

He was sweeping the corridors that led from the precinct to the storerooms, thinking about Raden and his wanderings through the kingdom, and thinking also about Princess Tashala and the unguents she had soaked into her hair — treacle? Beef fat? Butter and sugar? What had she taken to him? — when Hart and Quath appeared from the linen cupboards at the other end of the passage. Their arms were piled high with fresh sheets and blankets. When they saw Gan, they both laughed and dropped their voices into a hearty mutter.

"Afternoon, Gan," Hart said with a curl of his lip as they passed. "Or should that be 'Prince Janna' …"

Quath guffawed loudly and buried his mirth in the pile of sheets he bore. Gan leaned on his broom and kept his eyes level with them.

"Janna?" he said lightly. "I am not king yet, but I have no doubts you'll both be my subjects one day."

Hart, squat and lumbering, shook his head and squared himself against the slighter boy. The sheets he carried were a barrier between them.

"What gives you such balls to think like this, eh?" he spat. He pushed with the pile of sheets, and Gan stumbled back, dropping his broom. "You'll no more be the abbot than I will. I know my worth, and the place it gives me. I am content with it. But the Egg sees you, Gan, always chafing at the bit. Even if you can't see yourself."

Gan swallowed. He tried to keep Hart's eye locked in his own, but of a sudden all the words of scripture he could have thrown back at the bigger boy fell away from him. A fist in the gut he would have expected, a twist of the arm and a knuckle in the eye, but not this scorn. This low blame, this angry disappointment. He had no weapon against it.

"You think the Egg sees me as Janna?" he said. He tried to sound light-hearted, but his voice felt thick in his throat. "I would have thought King Raden more appropriate, personally."

"And how do you figure that?" Quath giggled. "Raden was humble, wise. He did what he thought was right. So did Tashala. All you care about is looking better than anyone else."

"That's not true," Gan said. He could feel his cheeks flushing red.

"Look at him," Quath mocked. "It's finally sinking in … That's your problem, Gan. You know scripture, fine. But do you really *know* it?"

"Don't think yourself more than you are," Hart muttered. He took the weight of the sheets in one hand and jabbed a finger at him. "Suck the Egg's hair all you want, but you're not King Raden. Not even close. You're Janna, boy. Lost with desire, and led astray. Grabbing at what you don't deserve. The Egg couldn't *believe* you'd ask such a question and not see yourself in the answer. No one could."

It's a hard thing to see a truth suddenly revealed, especially when it's visible to everybody except yourself. Gan seemed to see the lines of the story reframe themselves, and the grasping, wheedling figure of Prince Janna fade into the background where he belonged. In his place stood Princess Tashala offering her hair to her father, and beside her was King Raden, saddened by what he had done even when he knew it had been done for the best of motives. He thought suddenly of his mother, twisting the dry reeds into lengths of twine. He saw his father, his face lined with exhaustion.

When Hart and Quath had trundled off down the corridor, chuckling to themselves at the victory they'd scored in rendering him speechless, Gan stooped to pick up the broom. He leaned against the wall until his heart had settled.

He thought of Janna, standing in the door to his father's cell, his breastplate rent with battle, his clothes drenched in the dust of the roads. Weak, grasping, arrogant. But for a moment, as Gan composed himself again, he wondered at the strange courage it would have taken for Janna to walk down into those dungeons. He had gone to stand before the only person who truly knew the depths to which he had sunk, to ask the man he had imprisoned for help. That was why Janna had let his father live, Gan thought. It had taken courage to show that humility, and he could not betray that courage by committing such a base act afterwards. At the very end, Janna knew his true merits at last.

He felt his heart twinge at the thought. Perhaps the story then was about Janna's humility? Perhaps that was why the Egg had decided to tell it, and why those white eyes had rested on him at the very end. Until they had experienced the humility of knowing their limits, nobody knew what they were really capable of. That went for Gan as much as for anybody else. And then the king, after revealing those limits to his son, and realising his own limits in turn, slowly made his way to Kilavastin …

In the name of the Path, he thought, raising his eyes to the ceiling. Tales were twisting things right enough. They always told more than you really understood.

Perhaps the Egg meant him to understand that he was like both Janna and Raden? Ambitious, callow, only aware of his limits after he had been humiliated? Realising only afterwards why he had been sent to Kilavastin in the first place – not to succeed, but to serve.

Then, as the words of the story swept through him once more, Gan knew that he might not be King Raden; but he was certainly not Prince Janna either ...

Later that evening, he made his way to the Egg's cell. He bore the tea things on their lacquered tray, the ebony pot and cup, the simple clay bowl of dried leaves, the little crock of honey.

The Egg sat at his desk, drawing a reed stylus down a scroll of manuscript as he traced the letters of the text. Gan boiled the water by the blackened copper stove. Soon the fresh fragrance of the tea filled the room. It was getting dark outside, and the flame of the dusk stroked the open shutters at the window. Gan lit the candle in the lamp by the abbot's elbow.

"You have something to say, novice?" the Egg said at last. His voice quavered in the silence, weaker than it had been that morning. Gan poured the black tea into the ebony cup, straining the leaves. He looked at the globe of the Egg's head, the thin skin wrinkled above the back of his neck, the glint of his white eye as he sidled his gaze around to look.

Could it be him? How old was he really? How old was the tale they had heard that morning, the tale of King Raden and Tashala's hair?

"Forgive my distraction, master," he said. He took the water pot from the flame, setting it aside on the brick and bowing his head. "Truly, you see all things. But all day I have been thinking of the story you told us this morning. The tale of King Raden."

"You should have been thinking of the Path, novice." The Egg looked at him more fully now, twisting around in his chair. Gan bowed, until his forehead was nearly touching the stone.

"Indeed master, forgive me. But the story ... it moved me more than I can say and I found myself lost in wonderings about King Raden, and whether he ever made it to Kilavastin. I have ever been a glutton for knowledge. It is my besetting sin." He stared up quickly at the abbot's face, peering closely at the eyes nestled there in their soft wrinkles of skin. "Of course, you must have known him yourself, master, when he came to Kilavastin ..."

There. A flinch, the twitch of a nerve in his ancient cheek. Was it? Gan could not be sure. He felt a pang of guilt that he had put the question to this wise old man, and then the guilt melted into the swirl of a wry affection. He thought of Hart earlier that day, calling him Janna. But he was not Janna, who had thought he wanted a kingdom, but in the end only wanted the glory of being king. Gan thought of his parents in their reed hut, and the *anernath*, and the chance that had placed him here in the heart of Kilavastin. If the abbot were to offer him any gift, he would surely turn it aside. His parents had not put his foot on the first rung of a ladder, one that would lead Gan to the head of the monastery. They had put his feet on the Path. The gift they had given him was the opportunity to learn. That was all, and that was more than enough. In the end, you had to accept what you deserved, not what you wanted. That was what the Egg had done, he was sure. All those years ago, he must have truly known his merits at last.

Gan felt himself wilting under the abbot's attention. After a moment the Egg turned aside and addressed himself to his manuscript again. The dusk had fractured now into shards of red and purple. The night was coming on. The only light in the cell was from the lamp at the abbot's elbow, the faint yellow glow of the flame in the copper stove.

"King Raden did not arrive at Kilavastin, alas," the Egg said.

"Then what happened to him, master?"

The abbot sighed. He seemed to deflate in the chair, like a pig's bladder with the air let out. He placed his stylus on the desk and folded his hands in his lap, still with his back to the room.

"King Janna lost his war, and lost the loyalty of his people. Princess Tashala killed herself when the *anernath* finally spilled into the grounds of the palace. Janna found her body lying in her chambers, the poison still bitter on her dying breath, and in his madness and grief he fled. He became a vagabond, flitting through the ruins of Sabaenea, hiding from his enemies until even his enemies had forgotten about him, assuming him dead. And then, one day, during his many and dangerous wanderings, he came at last across his father for the final time. King Raden was sitting at a wayside shrine, contemplating the Path, when a dusty, ragged beggar approached him. He saw that it was his son, much abused by the rigours of his journey. He remembered the words his son had said at their last meeting: 'Forgive me father. But if I ever see you again, I will kill you.'"

Gan raised his eyes. "And did he?"

The Egg shook his head; slowly, painfully. "No, for his father spared him even that. King Raden made no effort to defend himself, but submitted to where the Path had led him. He was a wise man, as we have said. He reached out for Janna's sword, and when Janna placed it into his hand, King Raden ended his own life rather than allow his son to become a murderer. And so that is the end of King Raden's story, and the end of every story where desire is the master. Sorrow, heartache, death."

"And what of Prince Janna?" Gan asked, a lump in his throat. He did not say it to the abbot, but the tale as told by his mother had never reached so far. He had always wondered what happened to the prince once the tale was done, but he could never have imagined this squalid death at a wayside shrine. For obvious reasons, it had not been thought fit for a child's ears, and as he heard the words it was as if Gan felt a last fragile part of his childhood wither away from him. Even the dream that he would one day sit in the abbot's place seemed no more than a childish fantasy that he was ashamed to have entertained.

The abbot stood up from the desk. Pain flickered like lightning across his face. He hobbled over to the bed, Gan skipping ahead of him to arrange the pillows so he could sit up and take his tea. On the meditation terrace, the Egg would never have answered these questions. The tale was told, and that was all there was to it. But here in his chamber, perhaps the precepts did not apply so rigorously. The law was, after all, made for men and women, and not the other way around.

"Prince Janna …" he groaned. "Ah, Prince Janna, who had been tossed this way and that by all the whims of his nature, whose hand had failed at everything it touched, and who had brought nothing but ruin and misery in his wake … What happened to Prince Janna, I wonder … What would a son feel who had been the cause of his father's death, and whose father had been nothing but kind and indulgent to him, who had forced his beloved sister into an early grave? Where would he go for peace and absolution? What of Prince Janna when he finally realised where his life had taken him, and what he had done ..."

Their eyes met. Gan bowed once more, his heart racing. The abbot closed his eyes, sat back on the pillows, the great bald head like a polished stone, the mouth bloodless and dry. Gan went back to the tea things and stirred in a spoonful of honey to the ebony cup. He brought it over to the bed and the abbot's eyes opened once more. It was getting dark now. The candle was burning low.

"Here, master," he said quietly, his heart overflowing. He held out the tea cup, offering it to him in all reverence. "Please. Sustain yourself."

See Richard Strachan's story "Tashala's Hair" online at Metaphorosis.
If you liked it, leave a comment. Authors love that!
Remember to subscribe to our e-mail updates so you'll know when new stories are posted.

About the story

The genesis of this story was something I read in Vishvapani Blomfield's biography of Gautama Buddha, about an imprisoned king who survived by licking the oils off his wife's body when she smuggled herself into his prison. The power of that story made me think about the way it might have been used, as a parable or a teaching aid, and then as the story altered in my mind I started thinking about the kind of monastic society that would use it as a means of instruction. I've always liked stories-within-stories, so I wanted to embed it in a wider narrative. It would be a fable that the main character, Gan, wouldn't quite understand, even though he thinks the meaning is utterly clear at first. Only as he reflects on his own position in the monastery does he come to realise the true import of the tale.

A question for the author

Q: What's a typical writing day like for you?

A: A typical day for me starts as soon as I get back from dropping my daughter off at school, about 9am. If I'm working on something I've been commissioned to write, then I write solidly straight onto the laptop, with a brief break for lunch, until about 2.30pm, picking it up again in the evening. If it's something else, then a lot of that time is spent thinking or sketching notes, usually by hand. I always try to fit in a long walk in the middle of the day as well, no matter the weather — nothing gets the imagination working better.

About the author

Richard Strachan lives in Edinburgh, UK.

www.richardstrachan.com, @richstrach

Copyright

Title information

Metaphorosis June 2022

ISSN: 2573-136X (online)
ISBN: 978-1-64076-230-5 (e-book)
ISBN: 978-1-64076-231-2 (paperback)

Copyright

Publisher

Metaphorosis
a magazine of speculative fiction

Metaphorosis Magazine is an imprint of
Metaphorosis Publishing
Neskowin, OR, USA

Discounts available

Substantial discounts are available for educational institutions, including writing workshops. Discounts are also available for quantity purchases. For details, contact Metaphorosis at metaphorosis.com/about

Metaphorosis Publishing

Metaphorosis offers beautifully written science fiction and fantasy. Our imprints include:

Metaphorosis Magazine
Plant Based Press
Verdage
Vestige

You can also find us:
@MetaphorosisMag, @MetaphorosisRev, @Metaphorosis
www.facebook.com/metaphorosis

Help keep Metaphorosis running by supporting us at
Patreon.com/metaphorosis

See more about some of our books on the following pages.

Metaphorosis

a magazine of speculative fiction

Metaphorosis is an online speculative fiction magazine dedicated to quality writing. We publish an original story every week, along with author bios, interviews, and notes on story origins.

We also publish monthly print and e-book issues, as well as yearly Best of and Complete anthologies.

Come and see us online at magazine.Metaphorosis.com.

Plant Based Press

plant
based
press

Vegan-friendly science fiction and fantasy, including anthologies of the year's best SFF stories, from 2016-2020.

Chambers of the Heart
speculative stories
by
B. Morris Allen

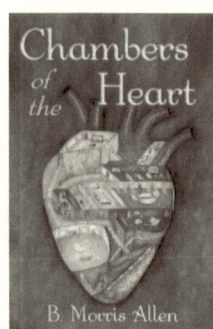

A heart that's a building, a dog that's a program, a woman sinking irretrievably — stories about love, loss, and movement.

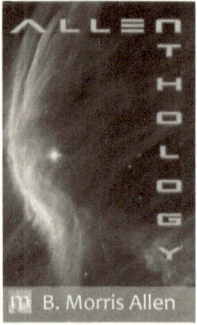

Susurrus

A darkly romantic story of magic, love, and suffering.

Allenthology: Volume I

Including three full collections of SFF stories.

Verdage

Science fiction and fantasy books for writers – full of great stories, often with an additional focus on the craft of speculative fiction writing.

Reading 5X5 x2

Duets

How do authors' voices change when they collaborate?

A round-robin of five talented science fiction and fantasy authors collaborating with each other and writing solo.

Including stories by Evan Marcroft, David Gallay, J. Tynan Burke, L'Erin Ogle, and Douglas Anstruther.

Score

an SFF symphony

An anthology with
an emotional score
from the heights of
joy to the depths of
despair – but always
with a little hope
shining through.

Reading 5X5

*Five stories, five
times*

See how different
writers take on
the same material.

Reading 5X5

Writers' Edition

Two extra stories,
the story seed,
and authors' notes
on writing.

Vestige

Novelettes, novellas, and novels by Metaphorosis authors.

The Nocturnals
Mariah Montoya

Night is Dangerous.
Day is deadly.

Where day and night last thirty years, humans move constantly stay ahead of the night and cruel Nocturnals that call it home. But a boy is lost out there.